# SHALMAR

## A Warrior's Tale II

### SERENA WHYND

ALL RIGHTS RESERVED
copyright © 2019 Serena Whynd
No part of this publication may be reproduced,
distributed or transmitted in any form or means, or
stored in a database retrieval system without the
prior written permission of the author. Circulation
of this book is prohibited in any format. This is a
work of fiction. Any resemblances of characters to
actual persons, living or dead, is not intentional and
entirely coincidental.

serenawhynd@protonmail.ch

Other Books by Serena Whynd:
**Phoenix Series**
The Paths That Be
Transcendence

**SHALMAR**
A Warrior's Tale I

# Table of Contents

# CHAPTER ONE

Shalmar watched the sun rise above the distant horizon as it cast numerous shadows of dark and light across the tall structures that made up the castle. She breathed in deeply, allowing her spirit time to recharge during this quiet hour.

She could hear the breath of her partner sleeping soundly. As Shalmar turned her attention to her companion, a streak of sun pierced through the window into the room and made a small halo on the helm of the fur rug they had slept on.

They were in Shalmar's quarters in the newly built wing allocated to the Amazons. It was a large room adorned with lavish furniture and decor, but to Shalmar, none of these things—gifts from Queen Natya and her royal council, were as beautiful as the woman that was stretched out still dreaming.

Jacqueline's face was veiled by her messy hair that flowed across her shoulders and settled on the small of her back just above the fur blanket that was draped over her thighs. Shalmar went to her quietly. With a slight movement of her fingers, she brushed the strands of hair from Jacqueline's face and leaned down to kiss her softly on her forehead. The smell of her hair, a pleasant fragrance of honey suckles, swarmed into her being.

Jacqueline made a gratifying noise in her sleep and Shalmar felt an aching throb in her groin. She slowly shook her head, blinking away the lustful thoughts that threatened to engulf her. With graceful movement of her naked body, she removed herself from the fur rug and went back to the window that overlooked the lay of the Amazon quarters.

With the end of the last war, Queen Natya, in her magnanimity, had commissioned the best painters in all Gilsk to paint and renovate most of the quarters of the Amazons, as well as the royal castle.

The queen had been in good spirits lately; it had been three days since the agreement with Yarael Twenty-Eighth to end the rivalry of their countries. As part of the celebrations, the queen had hosted a grand dinner for all the Amazons at the castle and personally thanked the warriors who were posted to the war fronts to fend off the enemies who had been gaining the upper hand.

Shalmar and Jacqueline had kept an eye on each other throughout the party. After expensive wine filled their cups, they both negotiated a quick benediction and snuck out of the castle and to her quarters.

Every time their bodies mingled in steaming passion, they always discovered something new. When Shalmar was with Jacqueline, she always felt like a wanderer exploring new places in the slender body of her young lover. She felt fulfilled in her partner's satisfaction every time a shriek of passion escaped Jacqueline's lips.

Shalmar stood by the window and marveled at the beauty of Blyst—the quietness of the morning, the splendor of the city walls, the elegance of the castle where their Queen resided—a soft sigh of relief escaped through her lips.

She heard the distant sound of weapons clanking, and her first instinct was to reach out for the penknife surreptitiously hidden under a chair. Her alertness settled when she remembered that it was common for training to commence early in the morning.

Her eyes wandered over to the south wing of the quarters where the Amazons usually trained. It didn't take long before she spotted a couple of her sisters at the grounds sparring with sizable swords and spears. It was a delight to watch an Amazon—their feet were light on the ground, their moves menacing. They sparred as though they were in the battlefield and their partner was an enemy to be defeated at all cost.

She watched as the trainee attempted to drive her spear through the blind spot of the other Amazon, dust rising from the ground as her feet pounded against it. For a moment, Shalmar feared the blade would pierce through the other woman, whom she presumed was an instructor from the black and bronze helmet she wore on her head. The instant the blade came close, the instructor swatted it away as though it was an annoying insect. She then danced to the left and head-butted the younger woman with the spear.

Shalmar watched as the spear flew at the girl's arm and she crashed to the ground.

She heard the echoes of encouragement and a warmness filled her heart.

Shalmar remembered the days when she was brand new to the Amazon way. She had noticed that preferential treatment had no place within the sisterhood of warriors—every warrior was treated equally, regardless of status. She noticed particularly that girls from noble families had something extra to prove; they were not to be regarded as weak. She had seen that resolve upfront with Jacqueline, the way she fought, the determination in her strides. For people from the streets like Shalmar, fighting came naturally; it had always been a part of her.

The way of the Amazons, she noted, was tough; they believed in building up independent, formidable, and fearless women who would work together within a team. Resilience was the key to survival here, and this place had always felt like home for as long as she could remember.

"A lovely view to wake to."

A familiar voice broke through her reverie. She smiled, turning to face her lover. Her eyes drowned in the depths of Jacqueline's blue ones.

"I wish we could spend the whole day locked up here. I do not think anyone will bother with us after the dinner last night."

Jacqueline was now sitting upright on the rug. Her gaze taking in Shalmar's athletic body and chestnut hair that hung loosely down her bare back. She smiled as she moved to stand beside Shalmar at the large window. A shiver ran through Jacqueline as they touched. Last night had been particularly ethereal for her. After enduring a lengthy dinner, she had signaled Shalmar with her eyes they should leave. The untamed passion they had shared last night was different from the few previous times their bodies had mingled in the sheets. An overwhelming feeling of euphoria had engulfed her, and she had ridden the waves of passion in a way deeper than she had ever known before. Now, she felt rejuvenated, reborn, like a phoenix rising from the ash.

"Whilst I am tempted to give in to your selfish desires, you temptress," Shalmar laughed, "someone will come looking for us."

Jacqueline watched as Shalmar walked to the corner of the room and slipped into her robe, loving the softness of her in this morning.

"Besides, I am feeling nostalgic."

"About what?" Jacqueline's curiosity peaked.

"The Gilsk war." Shalmar moved towards the unclad woman who was once again sitting on the rug. "You know that when this war lingered, we were both filled with a motivation to complete the task given to us from the Crown."

"Yes," Jacqueline reflected on it. "I still remember how that felt, battling with those blasted Zals, the Grall Swamp, and sneaking with the priestess into the palace of Yarael the Twenty-Seventh."

"You forgot to mention the mage,"

"Ah, yes, the mage," Jacqueline sighed. "It was a stroke of luck to have Yarael the Twenty-Eighth coming in at the right moment to break the hold Declavius had on us."

That was not the way Shalmar remembered it. She remembered being trapped by the powerful spell that oozed from the short little nuisance of a mage. She recalled being helpless, too weak to fight, as she stared at the lifeless form of King Yarael twenty-seventh. The situation was bleak. Shalmar remembered welling up with rage, which triggered an energy that coursed through her. The energy was so distinct, so powerful, she had never experienced it before. She knew it was a form of magic—she just wasn't sure how it happened. Just before the Prince, now King, crashed through the glass window into the tomb, she remembered altering the binding spell the mage had placed on her. She had broken the bind from the wall and retrieved her sword without the mage knowing.

"The adventure is still fresh in mind, as though it had happened last night. Now that the war has ended, I sense another evil coming. By All, I do not pray for it, neither do I wish it to happen, but I sense that it isn't over yet." Shalmar joined Jacqueline on the floor.

"And we will be here to put a stop to it, if it ever happens," Jacqueline raised her eyebrows in enthusiasm.

"Hmmm. Your confidence is intoxicating. From whence did it come?" Shalmar teased.

"From the greatest Amazon warrior, I know," Jacqueline fixed a hungry gaze on her partner's green eyes. "You, Shalmar."

As her eyes fell to linger on Shalmar's soft lips, her hands found their way to the back of Shalmar's neck and brought her face down to hers. Their lips collided in a slow, deep, soulful kiss. A lovely sound slipped out of their mouths as their bodies settled on the soft rug.

The air was charged with their romance as Shalmar's hand slid tenderly up the inner part of Jacqueline's lean thigh. The noise of clanking weapons grew louder, the two were so engulfed in the essence of each other they did not hear it. A rapping on the door brought them to a halt.

"Told you someone would come looking for us." Shalmar gave a slight frown as she stood up, adjusted her robe, and went to the door. Jacqueline grabbed her robe, drew it over her shoulders, and secured it into position.

Shalmar parted the door, enough to see whom the unwanted visitor was. She stared into the familiar face of Portia, a new addition to the Amazon Tribe. Portia, with a host of new recruits, was shortlisted for the last mission of retrieving the stolen Tarlaeth from the palace. Shalmar had her eyes set on Jacqueline, and Portia was then posted to fend off the enemy troops at the front lines. Portia straightened her stance and stood at attention.

"Portia, relax. What brings you here this morning?"

"I have orders from Command Tower,"

Command Tower was the building where the highest ranked officers from the Supreme Order of the Amazon Warriors were situated. The building towered over every other structure, offering a clear vantage point to survey the castle of the queen and the whole of Blyst.

Those at the Command Tower were mostly war strategists and planners who reported to the queen regularly on any impending war within the neighbouring cities, the outcome of the battle at the fronts, and preparation measures for a counter-offensive.

The success of the Amazon tribe at the front line was credited to the women who worked through the night to ensure the stability of the Gilskian troops.

Shalmar knew all the senior officers and got a chance to socialize with most of them during the dinner the queen organized the previous night. They all praised her and her partner for their feats of bravery. For some of them, the idea of a mage was a folklore that has been passed down from generation to generation. The reality of it, evidenced by Shalmar and Jacqueline, was overwhelming for some of them.

"Who requests my presence?"

"Commander Sym," Portia was trying to hide her smile. "She seemed to be in good spirits today."

"Why, if I may ask?"

"Can't place a finger on it. She requests your presence within the hour."

"Will that be all?"

"That will be all." Portia raised an eyebrow to Shalmar, and with a flirtatious grin, she nodded respectfully.

"I will be there shortly," Shalmar, aware of what just happened and showing no interest, closed the door.

Shalmar wondered why Commander Sym summoned her presence to the main post. The only time she was requested to meet with Sym was when there was a covert mission to be carried, like the mission to recover the magical statuette the Tarlaeth. She pondered as she moved into the room, could there be another mission?

Jacqueline noted the puzzled look on Shalmar's face. Shalmar informed her about the message that Portia relayed, and Jacqueline wondered aloud if another clandestine mission was imminent.

"That's what I intend to find out," Shalmar proclaimed.

They agreed to rendezvous later in the day. Jacqueline wanted to rush to her quarters and get dressed for training. Shortly after, Shalmar marched out of the room, fully dressed and curious.

# CHAPTER TWO

The room reserved for the Commander of the Amazon tribe, who doubled as the Leader of the Supreme Council, was a spacious office. Commander Sym stood at the corner of the office staring out the window. Watching the boisterous activity of Blyst, her lips stretched into a smile. Her dark hair was trimmed and tied at the top of her head with threads woven from leather. She had prominent cheekbones that accentuated the beauty of her oval face and intense brown eyes. Rumour had it that when she made direct contact with anyone, she would always get the truth from them.

Sym was approaching the late stages of middle age, even though her features appeared young. She had fought in the battlefield in the days when the queen rose to power. When the queen had claimed the throne after the death of her father, the male rulers of the nearby villages of Koron and Karneig saw an opportunity to extend their rule and their lands to Blyst and all Gilsk. They were taught the hard way, in the most unfortunate of circumstance: the queen and the Amazons were not to be trifled with.

It came as a surprise to them when the Amazons, blessed with superior power, enviable weaponry, and a tactic second to none, countered their offensive and laid waste to their armies. The Amazons at the war front, under the direction of Sym, pushed the retreating opposition out of all the lands of Gilsk. The enemies would have destroyed their lands if not for the swift intervention of Sym, who didn't want to anger the fates and the mighty All. Not a single Amazon warrior lost her life, and never again were such devious plans to overturn the supremacy of the Gilskian queen concocted.

Commander Sym didn't concern herself with the bureaucracies of the Command Tower. She only longed to be in the grounds, ensuring the peacekeeping treaty was maintained. She was a warrior, meant to be at the fronts. But she slowly rose up the ranks and was appointed a member of the Supreme Council of the Order. She was then quickly appointed as new Commander after the death of her predecessor.

Since then, Sym, together with the other members of the Supreme Order, had been involved in drafting new strategies for the Amazons to fend off other enemies of the Continent.

Since the return of Shalmar and Jacqueline and the end of the war, Sym had been elated. She had read through the reports that her subordinates submitted. Prince Yarael was a master strategist and was also in the field organizing a counterattack. She was losing her sisters and the men they had cajoled to be in the battlefield. The return of Shalmar and

Jacqueline was the coup de grace she needed to stifle the war once and for all.

Since their return, the queen had promised to renovate the Amazon quarters, and she had kept to her word. Today, she had promised to pay a sizable sum of gold to the blacksmiths stationed at the Amazon school to craft the best of blades and arrows for the warriors. Sym had been instrumental in revealing the identity of the inside person who had released the statuette—who turned out to be the queen's sister, Trupya. Sym was particularly pleased that the queen had made the decision to lock Trupya in her room till death took her. She had never liked the arrogant brat that paraded herself as a Gilskian princess, simply because royalty flowed through her veins.

Sym knew that a chunk of the praise went to the two brave heroes who had crossed enemy lines, dealt with dangerous creatures, and unfavourable weather—all for the greater good of everyone in Gilsk and, by extension, the continent.

She heard a knock at the door, which jarred her thought process.

"Proceed," she said, loud enough for the visitor to hear through the door. Shalmar opened the door and slipped into the office. As their gazes met, Shalmar gave a brief salute and closed the distance between them.

"Commander," Shalmar's voice was full of formality. "You sent for me?"

"Yes, I did. Please, have a seat," she gestured to a chair in the office.

When Shalmar was fully settled, Sym drew up the other seat across the table and sat down. Shalmar sat at attention, looking at Sym as she stared back for longer than was necessary. Sym was impressed with the warrior that sat across from her. She was particularly pleased that some of the unthinkable maneuvers that Shalmar had pulled off over the years were still being studied and practiced in Amazon training. She was staring at a legend, and a young one, at that.

"I have sent for you because I have important information, I'd like to share with you," Sym said, her voice smooth and calm.

Shalmar, skilled in the knowledge of conversation, remained silent, waiting for Sym to continue her speech. Seeing that Sym was not ready to spill the information, she offered, "A mission?"

She watched the commander part her lips into a gentle smile.

"No. Not a mission."

Sym was a keen observer. It was part of her many gifts. She realized the warrior was somewhat disappointed with her reply. Sym handled the situation quickly.

"It is not a mission, but it is equally as important," Sym's rose to her feet.

Shalmar felt compelled to stand up, but Sym gestured for her to remain seated.

"I have seen your records," Sym directed herself towards the window, her back turned to the seated warrior. "Right from your recruit days, you have demonstrated strength and resilience that is still being recognized and even taught by the instructors at the school."

Hearing this from a superior officer made Shalmar flush. Shalmar knew she was dedicated to the core values of the Amazons. That dedication was unwavering even in the bleakest of situations. Listening to the Commander say the same thing she had always known about herself felt amazing, almost as amazing as when she was within a breath of her partner—almost.

"The Warrior of Rheyn," Sym said, her back still facing Shalmar.

*The Warrior of Rheyn* had been an unofficial title Shalmar had been fondly called by her Amazon sisters and most of the folks from the small town. She was undecided about the name, as it made her remember how troublesome the town of her birth was.

"Yesterday, before the dinner the queen had organized for us, I read through your reports for the Tarlaeth mission. I was impressed with the masterful and quite unorthodox decisions you made along the way."

"I was only doing the best of my duties," Shalmar offered. "It is nothing worthy of your praise."

"Do not say it is nothing," Sym turned to face the warrior. "I have been in the fold longer than anyone alive, I have never seen such strategies employed by anyone before. It can only be pulled off by a master strategist." A smile appeared across her face.

A thought lingered in Shalmar's mind. She wasn't sure of it, but she thought she knew where the conversation was tilting. She just needed to hear it from Sym.

"Yesterday during the dinner, the members of the Supreme Order came to a decision. It was unanimous and, quite frankly, I had envisioned it for a long time now. Unfortunately, we couldn't proclaim the announcement because you were nowhere to be found."

Shalmar remembered how the members of the Supreme Order familiarized with her the previous night, she shifted in her seat, an uneasiness overwhelmed her. "I had retired early to my quarters." Shalmar found herself, momentarily, distracted by flashbacks of Jacqueline's nails marking her back. She brought her eyes to meet Sym's as she cleared her mind.

"I thought so." Sym gave a knowing smile. "Nonetheless, I have to tell you now." Sym leveled her gaze on the warrior. "There has always been a vacant seat in the Supreme Order for as long as I can remember. We have decided that it must be occupied by a warrior deserving of it. We selected you, Amazon Shalmar, Warrior of Rheyn, to occupy that seat."

Shalmar's thoughts had been confirmed. She stared at her commander, her eyes like gambler's—

stoic, revealing neither delightfulness nor disappointment.

"If you choose to accept our decision, you will be escorted to your new quarters, one specifically fitted to your unique needs. A guard, at your behest, will always be on ground, escorting you..."

Shalmar watched as Sym went on and on, reeling out the description of her duty, should she accept it. For a brief second, Shalmar thought about the prospects of becoming a member of the Supreme Order. It would be a huge shift from her life as a warrior. She would take a back seat from fighting in the war front. She would plan innovative strategies with other members of the order at the Command Tower to move the fold to greater heights.

"No," Shalmar said, cutting her commander off mid-speech. Shalmar's voice was loud and may have seemed insulting to her superior.

"No, thank you," she repeated calmly this time. "I have no intentions of filling a hallowed seat at the Supreme Order. I have never nursed such ambitions before, nor will I entertain such thoughts at this point." Shalmar knew that a life outside of fighting for her people at the fronts was not her life.

"Consider your decisions," Sym said softly.

"I have considered them." Shalmar met her gaze. "I want to remain in the service of the queen, but out there fighting with the team."

Sym looked away. "It is disappointing to hear this from you, but I do respect your decision, Shalmar."

"Will that be all?"

"Yes, that will be all." Sym proclaimed flatly.

Shalmar stood up, gave a short nod, and marched out of the room.

Sym watched as the door slid shut. She marvelled at the warrior who had just occupied the room with her moments ago. Her energy still filled the room as if she were still present.

Sym wasn't pleased that Shalmar turned down her request, but she was satisfied that the warrior assumed a prim appearance throughout their short discussion. She sighed as she turned to face the window, the sound of harps from the courtyard filling her ears.

She knew the Amazons would be in safe hands if they ever go into war again. With Shalmar at the lead, she was certain of it.

# CHAPTER THREE

The rest of the day moved on like pieces of debris picked up by a whirlwind. Shalmar had gone back to rendezvous with Jacqueline at the training grounds after the meeting with Sym. She needed to feel the thrill of fighting again. Shalmar took a little longer to get acquainted with the new tools the Amazons had instilled while she was on the mission retrieving the Tarlaeth. She loved the feel of her new sword in her hand, and she welcomed the burn in her muscles as she exerted physical force.

It was sundown now; the Amazons had retired to their quarters. Shalmar and Jacqueline were together, discussing her meeting with Sym. Jacqueline respected Shalmar had not accepted the offer to be a member of the Supreme Order. She knew she loved to be amongst the team. If she had accepted, it could pose some changes for them both as well. Their interactions and even contact would possibly be less. Shalmar would be occupied with her new role and others may feel Jaqueline would be favoured for certain missions. Shalmar and Jacqueline resolved that it was for the best that she had declined the offer. Jacqueline knew the brilliance of her partners mind and her skills. She was aware that having her in a position of such authority would be just as beneficial as having her physically with the Amazons at the front line. Jacqueline knew at some point, Shalmar would eventually take the lead of the Amazons with Sym and continue in that position well beyond Sym's time.

They were both cuddled under the long fur that draped over the rug on the floor; it seemed to be their choice for sleeping rather than the bed. Jacqueline nestled her head on Shalmar's chest and listened to her soft breathing. She was fast asleep. She had trained exceptionally hard, enjoying the feel of the new weapons in her hands.

Just before Jacqueline offered her body to the arms of sleep, she snuggled closer into Shalmar. It was where she felt best.

***

"Help. Help."

Shalmar was tossing in her sleep, lost in a dream. She was doing her best to adjust to this new environment. For one, the darkness was so profuse a blade could slice through it. All around, the darkness stretched on for miles.

"Help."

She heard the screams for assistance again, this time more heart piercing. Her hands wandered on their own volition to her sides. A dread swept through her when she realized that there was no weapon. She raced towards the sound. But the noise seemed to come from every direction, a low echo that projected endlessly.

As she charged forward, she met something hard and crashed to the floor. Raw pain shot through her. Her forehead throbbed as she struggled to her feet and felt the surface of what had broken her pace.

It was a wall, she assumed, as she ran her hands over the rough surface. As she moved forward, a hand jutted out of the wall and grabbed her arm. Its hold on her was firm and strong.

"You don't belong here," the voice reminding Shalmar of bones rattling.

A sudden paleness washed over her as she tried to untangle herself from the arm that held her in place.

Suddenly, as though awoken from a deep slumber, she heard the voices echoing in monotone: "You do not belong here. You do not belong here. You do not belong here."

The arm started persistently pulling her into the wall. She had never felt so terrified. Her body moved towards the wall, not fighting against the arm. She tried to steady herself. She wouldn't give up that easily.

With all the strength she could gather, she pulled backwards. The grip on her arm slackened. It gave her an idea and she pulled again, and she realized that its hold on her was no longer firm. With rage coursing through her, she balled her free hand, raised it above her head, and brought it down hard on the arm that held her.

It made a low wincing sound and retracted back into the wall. With some relief, Shalmar moved away from the barrier and started running in the opposite direction, her heart was pounding in her ribcage in erratic heaves. The monotone voices faded in the distance.

She stopped and caught her breath. She could still hear the scream for help, but it was faint now, as though the person screaming had given up and simply succumbed to whatever her fate was.

Shalmar heard galloping sounds before she spotted the horse in the distance, charging towards her. She saw it was a powerful beast, a creature of best health. She had never seen a horse so white, and she noticed the atmosphere change as it approached her. The horse had eyes like coals of fire, burning brightly and lighting up the path.

As the gap between them quickly closed, Shalmar observed the horse's rider. She couldn't see most of the face, for it was covered with a thick white cloak that flowed to their legs.

"Move no further," Shalmar braced herself.

The horse threw its head back, whinnied loudly, and halted in its tracks. She took some time to regard its rider. All she could see of their face were the green eyes that locked with hers. They seemed sad and filled with regret.

She could barely hear the cries for help reverberating in the background. Even though it was faint, she felt the need to act and render assistance to the helpless soul. She needed to know where she was, and this rider could have some answers. Just as she went to speak, the rider's voice broke the silence.

"I'm sorry to have brought you here, Shalmar."

She was surprised that the rider knew her name. His voice resonated with her in such a way she didn't understand. He had said her name with an unusual tone she was yet to place. It was as though he had known her all her life. What she had learned from Amazon training was to always remain calm even when plagued with uncertainties.

"Where am I?" She managed to level her voice.

"This is the chasm between life and death," the rider spoke. "It is the only place where I can speak to you, for I no longer walk the path of the living and my body has been laid to rest with my ancestors. It is not the case with you. You are neither dead nor alive here. You are only floating. Your body is back in your room. I will not fail to let you know that if you remain here for long, the dangerous beings that lurk in this murky void will drag you along."

She had previously experienced that firsthand, and she was not ready to entertain such dreadful feelings again.

"Your mate will soon discover that your body has gone cold and will try to wake you. I have little time." He adjusted himself in the saddle.

"Who are you? And what am I—"

"An unspeakable evil is imminent." She noticed the despondency in his voice. "The one whose blood you share is in grave danger from a threat to overtake the throne. You can hear her voice all around these walls, do you not? The evil needs to be stopped. It needs to be distinguished."

"I do not understand—"

"My time is short here." The gelding advanced slightly. "You must journey through the Western Sea to the Numinous Sea. Find the edge of the continent. Only then shall you find what was long taken from you. You will unravel this soon enough."

"What are you talking about?" Shalmar was trying to catch even a glimpse of his face.

As he went to speak, his voice was drowned out by the sound of a familiar voice that called to her.

"Wake up Shalmar, wake up."

Instantly, she felt a force she hadn't known before, beginning to pull her backwards. She tried to control it, but it only proved impossible. The rider removed his cloak to reveal his face, but he was too far for her to see him now.

"Wake up. By All, you must."

"Who are you?" she screamed as her body retreated farther from the horse and rider.

She was sure he was looking directly towards her, even though she couldn't spot his face.

"You already know who I am." She heard his voice in her head. "You already know who I am."

She woke up abruptly. Her vision was too blurry for her to see at first—her surroundings were just pale light with dark forms drifting across it. She felt cold water on her face and her vision cleared out. She coughed as she took in her surroundings, her head reeling around perplexed.

"What happened, Shalmar?"

Shalmar examined the worried face of her partner, and she released a huge sigh of despair. It was a strange feeling that had woken her; Jacqueline was terrified when the once warm chest she was laying on turned brumal in an instant. When she saw how pale Shalmar looked, she feared the worse had happened.

She had hefted her stiff frame beside the fireplace and had shaken her so violently that the cold began to dissipate from her body and the energy started to flow again.

"What happened, Shalmar?" Jacqueline brushed the dark bangs from her brow.

Shalmar fluttered her green eyes and it all came rushing back to the her. The chasm. The screams. The white horse and its rider.

"Evil is imminent," she whispered, repeating what the rider had said.

"Evil?" She could hear the confusion laced in Jacqueline's voice as she strained to sit upright on the floor. Her strength failed her, and as she began to struggle, she felt Jacqueline's hand firmly reach behind her to hold her in place.

"Yes." Shalmar took in a deep breath. "Another evil is drawing near. I do not understand most of it. But I had felt it long before now, this uneasiness that comes with peace. And now it has been confirmed."

"Shalmar?" Jacqueline examined her closely. She had not seen Shalmar this way before, and it worried her. She wasn't making sense.

Shalmar closed her eyes, remembering every line the rider had said, searching for details in his words, but she came up with nothing. It was frustrating.

Maybe it was just a bad dream, Shalmar mused. Maybe the nightmare was due to the stress she had exerted in the previous day. She knew it was much more than that. She knew it was just an excuse to draw herself away from the reality of what was to come if she didn't act upon it.

The rider only said a few things, but he had banked on her resolve to untangle the many knots that had been woven around this puzzle. She knew she wouldn't find any answers to the many questions in this room.

"I must go to Rheyn."

The statement seemed to catch Jacqueline off guard. It was the last place she had expected Shalmar to want to visit. When she looked in the depths of her partner's eyes, she knew that Shalmar was serious. It was a connection they had always shared.

"I will go with you." Jacqueline touched Shalmar's face and searched her eyes.

"I do not want you dabbling in matters I am yet to understand."

"That is reason why you need me by your side."

"There are more questions than answers, Jacqueline."

"We will find the answers together."

Jacqueline stood up and grabbed a fur blanket hanging beside Shalmar's armour and draped it over her shivering body. As Shalmar explained her dream and her need to return to Rheyn, she began to feel better. The fur was welcoming, spreading heat back into her body.

"Now," Jacqueline said softly. "You need to get some rest before we head out." She gently pulled Shalmar into the warmth and comfort of the large bed.

Pulling the covers up, Jacqueline stroked her hair and kissed her softly. She intended to let Shalmar sleep, but Shalmar reached up and pulled Jacqueline's slender frame onto her. As their mouths moved in a deliberate, lingering kiss, Jacqueline's senses were exploding brighter than any nebula in the heavens. Her hands and her mouth explored her partner's lithe figure. She caressed Shalmar with the intricate focus and precision of an artist yielding to the energy transcending from above. The energy met the canvas and created a masterpiece of emotion. She felt herself so mesmerized by the energy flowing between them it was almost debilitating. She could feel Shalmar quiver with each touch, with each pattern her lips left on her smooth skin. As Jacqueline slowly returned to kiss the sweet mouth of her partner, their gaze held. The silent conversation between them was of an intimacy stronger than any words could convey. With a slight move of her slender thigh, Shalmar invited her in. Jacqueline felt her heart fill with a love and devotion so freeing and so aligned. She knew Shalmar had never been so open, so vulnerable, and in being so, Shalmar had never been more powerful. She moved respectfully to her place and with every stroke of passion they shared, Jacqueline tonight was the maestro and Shalmar her song.

# CHAPTER FOUR

In the pitch darkness that enveloped the quiet meadow, crickets chirped happily, their sound piercing the stillness of the night. A strange but comforting wind blew across the vast acreage of the land, caressing the tips of leaves, swaying them back and forth.

At the far right of the meadow, close to the bank of the small lake, stood a lonesome hut. Two figures moved slowly and mindlessly inside, chatting with their voices barely audible for anyone else to hear.

"I have a duty to my people," one of them said, facing the other. "We must leave at the first stroke of dawn."

Under the glow of the small lamp in the room, the man looked aged. Worry lines, like henna, ran across his forehead. Parts of his upper body were shrouded under the cloak he wore. The cloak flowed from the top of his head down to the ground to his sandals.

It was a ceremonial cloak, made of the finest satin sewn together by maidens who lived in lands miles away from where the hut was located. Whoever adorned a cloak like this was a notable member of the royal family, if not the crown bearer.

His gaze was fixed on the hazel eyes of the powerful woman that faced him.

"If we leave now, take the two geldings who are well rested and fed. We can carry enough supplies. We'll get to Jadehollow before dusk in three days. It'll be a long journey, my love, but it will be wort—"

"You will go without me," she spoke softly, but firmly, cutting him off mid-speech. "I always knew this day would come. You have your duty as I have mine." She let her gaze fall to the ground as she turned her back to him.

"Sarith, you have to—" He wanted to make her see things from his perspective.

"Right from the night our worlds joined, when you drew me into your deep embrace, it had always lingered. I had turned a blind eye to it all."

"This is why we should go together. I feel deep in my gut that something has happened while I sojourned here. Be with me, my love. You are my primary mate. Live with me in a land where you will be respected and loved."

"What about our children?" Sarith asked, without turning to face him. She was staring at the door that led into another room. "The real question is, what about Shalmar?"

Whatever he was about to say clamped back into his throat as the question Sarith raised caught him off guard. He rolled the question over in his head as he let his eyes follow her gaze. Even though the door was shut tight, his ears could pick up the short intermittent bursts of air coursing through their lungs.

Their two girls were sleeping peacefully as children should.

"You said it yourself," Sarith turned to face him. Her eyes no longer held the fire he once saw in them. The energy they had shared in the few years they'd been together was going through its last phase of existence, its essence dissipating.

"Ruther," she spoke softly. "You told me you felt that untapped energy flowing within Shalmar. She belonged here, fated to be an important member of the Order of the Amazon Warriors. I can feel it too. I see it in the way she protects her younger sister from harm. I see it in her green eyes—your eyes. And I have a deep resolve that the destiny that awaits her in Jadehollow isn't hers. I cannot let that happen."

Ruther held her piercing gaze and, for a moment, he remembered the first time they had crossed paths.

He was just like every other young man in Jadehollow—wild and adventurous—even though royalty from ages past coursed through his veins. His father, the king of Fellnesia, Jadehollow, and all the lands that made up the Air Element, wanted him to settle down. He wanted him to get united with a maiden who would be his primary mate and begin to plan his ascension to the throne in the event of his death. Ruther would have none of that. He would not disrespect the king's wishes as it would be considered a heinous crime, treason, but he was always motivated by an earnest desire to sojourn to a land different from their own. He was Air after all. He also felt within him that the one to be his primary mate was not in these lands.

On a fateful day, just before the cock crowed, he removed himself from his kinfolk and set out. He made sure to stay off the main paths, aware that his father would send his best men out looking for him. He had more of a chance not to be seen if he used the lesser trails.

Several days passed, and he knew the scouts had gotten tired of the search and returned home to report to the king of their failed quest. With the deep connection shared between the two, he could feel his father's disappointment. He could also sense another energy pulling him forward and he couldn't deny his need to follow it. He knew, though the king was troubled with his disappearance, his father was reassured with the idea that he was alive and breathing.

He moved through the lands—Koron, Karneig, Borr—taking notes of the various civilizations ensconced in them. He never stayed long, at least not long enough to make any acquaintances in each of the cities the fates led him to. Whenever he began to feel he was settling, he would move to the neighbouring city or town.

It was the fates that had led him to that meadow just a short distance from Rheyn, a town of Gilsk. He spotted Sarith as she was roasting an antelope, she had killed with one of her arrows. She looked intimidating—he had never seen a woman wield so much strength and resilience throughout the lands he had toured.

He couldn't understand it just yet, but he knew the fates had directed his steps to that meadow for a reason.

Sarith had been aware of his presence long before he spotted her. She was an expert hunter, trained to pay attention to the little details—changes in the temperature, unnatural noises—by the best hunters in Gilsk. She had always wanted to be an Amazon. She loved the way they were precise and thorough. Instead she was handpicked to go through hunter training. She was a natural and quickly became the best at her art. Her reputation known through many towns.

While she lived in Rheyn, a troublesome part of Gilsk, she had kept a hut at the meadow as a haven, not more than an hour away from the rancour of the town. Here, she kept the spoils of her kill and sold them to the traders at the coasts of Blyst, the capital city. She knew the importance of a sane mind and body, and by All, she was going to keep it that way.

When Ruther approached her formally and met her acquaintance, she knew he was different from all the men she had known in Gilsk and in all the lands that surrounded the banks that connected Midbay. Though he appeared somewhat wild, she knew deep down he was noble, and he possessed an air around him that she had never felt before. He had appeared before her as she was hauling some water up the hill. After she refused his help, he was determined to sit in front of her home until she spoke with him. When seeing him there in the morning, she told him he can assist her with her hunt.

Their mutual fondness grew, and they shared several strokes of unbridled passion. Soon after they first met, Sarith birthed a beautiful baby girl, and they were blessed with another girl two years later.

That was when Ruther began to sense an energy that he could trace back to the land he had abandoned several years previous—Jadehollow. The energy was of sorrow and pain. He knew what he was sensing was his father's passing. He could hear the calls for him to return. He was trying to convince Sarith to come with him, with their children, to the land of his birth.

Ruther stood in the room with a sombre-faced Sarith. He knew that the best of his lifetime had been spent with this exceptional huntress, and it was heart-breaking that it might all go away. But he had a duty to his people—to Jadehollow—and he knew his time here had come to an unavoidable end.

"You told me," Sarith repeated, stepping closer to slip her hand through the cloak to caress his face. "Shalmar's fate has been aligned with the Amazons, and you can see a bit of yourself in Fernella. I can feel it, too. I have seen Shalmar's rise to greatness."

"Yes. Their fates are undeniable," he whispered, barely audible as he knew this woman who held his heart and soul forever was right in her choices.

Their eyes held again, and a connection passed between them. They both understood what needed to be done. However, neither of them could summon the courage. It was a difficult decision; it would split their small family in half, and from all indications, it was possible that they would never cross paths again in this lifetime.

"We agree. Shalmar will remain with you, while I take Fernella to Jadehollow," Ruther could barely recognize his own voice. "With Shalmar here, Fernella will one day become ruler of the Air Element, taking my place at the throne." Ruther blinked back the tears trying to burst from his eyes, he walked past her and entered the room.

It was dark, but the light that poured in from the adjacent room made him spot the girls easily. There was a thick fur rug on the floor. On it, the two girls lay sound asleep, their breath filling his ears. He moved slowly, as he wanted this moment to last. He moved to the edge of the rug, and slowly knelt beside Shalmar. She, their eldest child, was beautiful and graceful, even in her floating state.

He started chanting, his voice petered down to a whisper; he couldn't risk waking them up with his voice. The risks were enormous and the moment dire. He had learnt this act a long time ago, from his father and he from his father before him. It required patience, which he wasn't sure he possessed. But he closed his eyes and kept on with his ritual, spreading his arms over the sleeping child and muttering in a language that none of them had ever heard before.

Soon, he began to feel the energy rising from his core towards the tips of his fingers. The energy coursed from his being and settled in his face. His eyes peeled open and they were no longer grey-green; a bright white-purple light glazed over them. He fixed his gaze on the sleeping child and touched her forehead with both his hands.

A jolt of energy shot through her, jerking her body, almost making her stumble awake. He felt the essence of the Air element slipping into his first-born child and a sadness he hadn't known before filled him. He also knew the power she possessed; he knew she would be a force of her own and for the Amazons. He had seen it in a vision.

When he was satisfied that enough energy had transferred to Shalmar, he shut his eyes and the connection severed. She still looked so graceful in her sleep, and he knew that from that moment, everything was going to change. He swooped his head and kissed their daughter's forehead.

"Goodbye, Shalmar," he said soulfully, tears slipping out from his eyes. "Maybe one day you'll understand the implications of what just happened tonight. Maybe one day you'll forgive my actions and open your eyes to see the bigger picture."

Ruther stood up and walked around to where the other child was. Fernella was smiling in her sleep. She was the one he had to guide and protect now. She was the one who belonged to Jadehollow, the place of his birth, the land of her ancestors.

He grabbed the sleeping child into his arms, making considerable steps not to wake up her older sister, Shalmar. Slowly, he dragged his feet solemnly across the room to find Sarith waiting.

"Damn the fates," A sadness hovered in her eyes and flowed through her voice. "Stay here with m—"

"My duty has to be for my people now," Ruther said as he approached the woman to which his heart belonged. "I must go get a horse."

He placed the child in her arms and walked out of the hut, into the night air. The sky above mirrored the colour of his heart, a hollow where happiness once was.

He stumbled to the back of the hut where the shed was located. It was a makeshift stable he had singlehandedly built many summers ago. He grabbed the reins of the first gelding he saw. He had packed supplies and strapped them to the horse, and from all indications, the horse seemed prepared for the journey ahead. Ruther walked with the horse back to the front of the hut. Sarith was waiting for him, her eyes watery with tears.

She handed the sleeping child to him reluctantly after kissing her forehead and staring at her lovingly. Before he turned, she reached out and removed the cloak from his head and parted his lips with hers. It was a slow and sad movement of their lips. She was not ready to see him leave. The reality of raising a child on her own troubled her; more so, the thought of her husband and younger child leaving was another pain she couldn't bear.

She slowly removed her lips from his. "Promise me," her voice lacking vigor. "Swear on it. Fernella will be well taken care of."

"By All, I swear." His eyes never leaving hers. "On my life, I will look after her. I will guide her in the ways of Fellnesia. I will guide her until she becomes a princess, strong and compassionate, just like the woman who birthed her."

"As do I," Their hands touched. "I will take Shalmar to Blyst on the morrow and ensure she trails the path of her destiny."

He kissed her forehead and turned to climb the horse. The gelding grunted in displeasure, but it remained still. Ruther placed the child in front of him, straddling the horse and wrapping her tightly in his cloak.

Sarith stood rooted at the front of the hut, her eyes transfixed on her lover and child. She didn't doubt his promise; she could see that he would do anything to see her safe. She watched him grab the reins of the horse and command it to move.

His eyes held hers. "Shalmar will not have any memories of me, lest she risk her destiny of greatness and go in search of me. Do not tell her about me or whence I had come, although a part of me and my essence now lives in her. I love you, Sarith. I will always be with you both."

He shifted the horse to leave. The horse picked up speed and galloped away. Even in the darkness, Sarith hoped she would catch a glimpse of his face.

He didn't turn back. She never saw him or her younger child again. Nor did she see the tears streaming down his face, as he knew the best times of his life were passed.

# CHAPTER FIVE

The town of Rheyn, located many hours from the city of Blyst, was brimming with life, the midday sun blasting high in the sky. The two Amazon warriors and their horses galloped through the gates leading to the town. They maneuvered the horses through the market just inside the town gates and watched as the merchants standing beside their displayed goods called out to prospective customers.

As soon as people spotted the Amazons, the whole market went silent—it was as though their mouths had suddenly been sealed shut.

Shalmar, who rode slightly in front, gently pulled back on the reins and brought her horse to a gentle halt. A strange feeling crept down her spine as silence hung in the air.

Jacqueline brought her horse to a stop beside Shalmar. Neither of them were sure what to expect, so they did only what they were trained to do in an unusual turn of event—be prepared for anything. A silence like this could only mean one thing: something of importance was about to happen. Jacqueline's hands slithered to the scabbard that held her sword. She didn't pull the weapon out, but she wanted the weapon within reach, just in case.

Shalmar surveyed each of onlookers—their eyes, their faces—and she noticed that they all wore the same expressions of astonishment. The silence trailed all along the main road that channelled into the smaller roads that connected the alleys and boroughs of the town. She didn't feel any concern for their safety, but she didn't understand why everybody had gone quiet.

Suddenly, a cheer went up at the same time from every direction. The men raised their little children and placed them on their shoulders as they whooped happily. The women and young girls did a little dance, as they all chanted:

"The Warrior of Rheyn. Our own warrior."

Realization, like a rushing wind, hit the two Amazons. The people of Rheyn must have known about the recent exploit of Shalmar who was from their town. Even though she knew that rumours travel fast, Shalmar never believed the news of her covert mission would have reached here so quickly.

The lords who presided over the several districts of Gilsk were present when the queen had announced the impressive report the Supreme Council of the Amazons had submitted. Even though some details of their mission were left out, the lords filled in the blanks themselves and clearly passed the information to their families who then spread the news.

Even though they cheered and danced at the sight of the Amazons, no one dared to venture forward to have physical contact with them. It was an unspoken rule they all adhered to. When the Amazons guided their horses to start moving again, the people parted the road for them to glide through, and the warriors gave the people smiles and respectful nods as they passed by. Soon after, the whoops petered out and the usual activities resumed, as though nothing had happened.

Jacqueline was quite elated through it all. She was proud of Shalmar. The success of the mission had also caused Jacqueline to become popular in the small part of the city where she was born as well. Her parents, nobles of high repute, who lived in one of the most beautiful parts of Blyst, were proud of her exploits in the short period of time she had been a part of the sisterhood of warriors. She was quite hopeful that soon enough the whole of Blyst would recognize her as their own as Rheyn had done for Shalmar.

Jacqueline's gaze collided with Shalmar's. For a moment, all seemed to stand still. The knowing smile that came across Shalmar's face ignited the desire Jacqueline was still relishing from the wee hours of morning. The confidence and strength that moved from within Shalmar, Jacqueline found even more intoxicating since experiencing her essence to the depths that she had before sleep had finally came upon them. Shalmar shifted her attention back to her quest, a side of her still aching to be next to Jacqueline's warmth.

Shalmar was quite pleased that the town of Rheyn had honoured her the way they did. If her memory served her right, it was only a couple of moons ago that she, together with her partner, had followed a trail of thieves who had stolen the hallowed Tarlaeth to this very place. And the way they treated them now was a stark opposite of the reception they had received when they had charged through the town seeking information.

She scanned the town walls and noticed how they were like the walls that stood over the capital city. Even without attesting it, she knew the people of Rheyn shared some likeness with the people that lived in Blyst. Every now and then, there was bound to be an act of thievery or violence that can only be stifled by the appearance of an Amazon warrior.

Trotting through the streets, Shalmar felt warmth in her heart. Even though most of her life was spent where the Amazons trained and at the war fronts, the town connected her to the only family she had ever known.

This was why the dream had felt strange to her. She could hear the rider's voice reverberating in her mind; she had committed every word he had said to memory. She needed to confirm her beliefs. She wasn't about to venture off to the end of the continent because someone in a dream had appeared to tell her so. She had to follow her instincts.

They directed the horses into an alley and ensured that they maintained a slow and even pace. She knew the horses must be tired from riding most of the day. She was thankful Jacqueline had insisted on following her here. Not that she couldn't handle the matter herself, but her presence was welcome. If their positions had been flipped, Shalmar knew she would have done the same.

Shalmar pulled up on her reins and brought her horse to a stop in front of a small house. She gracefully dismounted the gelding and looked up at Jacqueline. Shalmar extended her arm to her partner, who grabbed it firmly and jumped down.

"What is this place?" Jacqueline was scanning around for movement.

Shalmar smiled softly. "This is the home of my mother. My home. Let's go in."

Jacqueline scanned the entrance of the building and noticed that there were metal chains that seemed to seal off the small property.

"Your mother does not appear to be home?"

She watched as Shalmar fished in the small leather pouch she had brought along and pulled out a small steel chain with a couple of keys attached.

"Not since her passing several years ago," her tone was low.

She moved forward to unlock the entrapments and push the door open. Dust filled their nostrils as the door opened wide. Even though the sun had begun to make a slow descent to set in the horizon, the clear sky outside offered enough lighting for them to see the contents of the house.

A bow made of the finest materials sat in the corner of the small room. A quiver slept beside it, containing enough arrows to take down an abundance of prey. All were covered in a thick layer of dust. The room was just the way Shalmar had remembered it.

It was only missing the powerful entity who once resided in it.

Jacqueline studied her partner as she scanned the room. From all indication, Shalmar was looking for something. But what was it?

What bothered her most was the sadness laced in Shalmar's voice when she proclaimed that her mother had died. She knew Shalmar was putting on a brave face, even though, deep down, she could feel Shalmar's poignancy.

Jacqueline didn't know how to respond to the comment for she had never lost any loved ones. She moved towards Shalmar and placed her hand on her shoulder, keeping it there as she could feel Shalmar relax with her touch. For the first time, when Shalmar turned to face her, she could see the tears threatening to flow down her cheeks.

Shalmar had never felt this vulnerable before. It was unusual for her, but this vulnerability was not of powerlessness. This feeling came with the inevitability of the changing hands of time. She attempted to blink back the tears as she gazed into the blue eyes of her partner.

"My mother, Sarith, was a powerful huntress," Shalmar smiled. "From the few tales she told me, she had always wanted to be a member of the Order of the Amazon Warriors. As fate would have it, she was exceptionally gifted with hunting and was instead selected to become a hunter. She was one of the best from what I have been told. Stationed to Rheyn, she toured the neighbouring forests of Borr and Koron, and caught dangerous beasts, which she then sold to traders at the bay. She had a small boat that she paddled into strange waters to catch fish, too. Her reputation was well known, as she was one of the best and most powerful trackers, able to take down anything she attempted to. She taught me all she knew. Those who speak of her say she was gifted by the Goddess Artemis. She was a master of her skills and none could surpass her."

"She must've been a brave woman." Jacqueline touched her cheek. For a moment, Shalmar pressed her face into Jacqueline's palm.

"The bravest woman I have ever known," Shalmar nodded proudly.

"What of your father?"

The experienced warrior wasn't expecting the question, so she let it hang in the air between them. Jacqueline, seeing the expression on Shalmar's face as she stepped away, knew it to be a tough subject.

"My mother never talked about the man who was my father. She avoided it altogether, a sadness always appeared whenever I pressed for information."

She began to walk around the room. "Talking about my father to me was an abomination for her. She kept the silence until it followed her to her death. But she didn't have to tell me about the man she offered her body to. From the way she always looked away whenever I pressed for details, I decided to sum up a conclusion about him through the years. A conclusion that has made it easier for me to understand why he would leave my mother alone and to fend for their child and…" Shalmar's gaze drifted off as she continued, "and why he didn't take us with him."

"And what would that be?" Jacqueline noted the pain in Shalmar's voice and watched as she regained her composure.

"That he was chicken-hearted." Shalmar raised her voice slightly. "That he was a destitute who wormed his way into my mother's heart and took advantage of the love she felt for him. A lowlife who would flee at the sight of a woman conceived with child afterwards. He would never come back to see the birth of his child, to see her be a part of the Amazons and to become a force to be reckoned with."

An anger filled Shalmar's eyes as she levelled her gaze with Jacqueline. "I curse the day fate brought their paths together." Shalmar shifted her eyes away from Jacqueline, careful to not have the anger she was feeling be misdirected at her.

As if on cue, a strong wind blew into the room, making all the boxes clatter noisily. It lasted barely a second, but Jacqueline felt a shiver go down her spine.

Complete silence fell on the room when Shalmar spoke. Jacqueline stared at her partner, curious that the wind came up with the emotion Shalmar had expressed. Shalmar wasn't frustrated anymore but the sudden hush of the room seemed to unnerve Jacqueline. In her gut, she knew there was a connection between Shalmar's emotion and the movement of the wind. Jacqueline had always felt energy flow through Shalmar, and now knew for certain, that there was more to this woman who had captured her heart.

"Shalmar?" she examined the warrior who was staring wistfully at the bow and quiver at the corner of the room.

"Coming here," Shalmar turned around looking at the home. "I had hoped to find some answers to the questions that have recently crippled my thoughts."

"You're referring to what happened last night and this morning?"

"Yes." It was still fresh in her mind, and as she reflected on everything, she felt discouraged.

"Tell me again." Jacqueline paid rapt attention as Shalmar spoke, their eyes holding as they relived the dream. The details were overwhelming. Jacqueline couldn't have imagined that there was such a place as the chasm between life and death.

"That is why it doesn't make sense to me," Shalmar was perplexed. "My only family, my mother, is dead. I have gone through her room and I don't know if what the rider discussed was really imminent or if I was just having a nightmare."

"I don't think it was a nightmare," Jacqueline had contemplated the potential outcomes. "We just have to dig some more. Go through her things. Maybe she kept something to figure out this puzzle. Maybe we are looking at the obvious. What if this dream has to do with your father?"

Shalmar's eyes held hers. It was a thought that had not occurred to her. She was appreciative of Jacqueline's partnership.

They examined every part of the small house looking for clues. It was a rigorous process. They didn't know what they were hoping to find, but Shalmar had an inkling that if they found it, it would be obvious.

The sun had dropped lazily, the light the sky offered was not enough for them to see inside. The warriors were tired and famished after their long day of travelling and searching the house.

Shalmar grabbed the only lamp, which sat the in one of the corners of the room. She wanted to light it up, then realized that it contained no oil.

"What do we do now?" Jacqueline yawned. "Do we start preparing to wait the night here or go back to town centre? We do have supplies and some food."

Even though spending the night in her mother's house seemed like the obvious option, Shalmar didn't want to. The house contained memories of many things she didn't want to dwell on.

Jacqueline, for the most part, was grateful that Shalmar was finally confiding in her about her past. It was overwhelming to hear her pouring out details, but she wanted to help Shalmar in any way she could. Jacqueline felt she had exposed her blind spot, and now it was her job to let Shalmar know she was safe with her.

"We can't sleep here."

There was a finality in her tone. She extended her arm for Jacqueline who took it and felt its warmth. She followed her outside the house.

"Let's get a drink and a hot meal. Then we can decide."

Shalmar thought about it briefly. In all Rheyn, there was only one inn. The owner wouldn't be too pleased to see them there, she mused.

"Let's go."

They gathered their horses that had been grazing and resting, neither creature looked happy to be moving again.

# CHAPTER SIX

The Old Bart was a pub situated right at the centre of town. Rumour had it that the owner, Nob, wanted a meet-point between those coming into the town from the north, Blyst, and those coming from the south, Makreh and Koron.

It was sundown, and the worn pub was filled to the brim with folks who were too drunk to retrace their steps back home. It was a large space with tables and chairs filling the room. Beside the bar, there was a small stage where a musician was confidently playing the lyre. A couple of drunks were raising their voices and they were soon exchanging blows, a nightly ritual within this drinkery. The other folks in the pub just stared absentmindedly as they fought.

Nob, the innkeeper, watched from the counter and was far too tired to separate them. A glass of mead was clasped between his hands, and that was the only thing that mattered to him.

In the heat of the noise, the door blew apart and the two Amazon warriors strode in. Almost immediately, the rancor petered down, and complete silence engulfed the pub—the men fighting on the ground froze in their stance, even the musician quickly stood up and removed himself from the stage.

The only sound that pierced the air was the creaking of the chairs as the drunks shifted in them.

The Amazons made a beeline to the counter and caught the gaze of the half-drunk barkeeper. He didn't hide the displeasure from his face. Nob had heard the rumours of how the Amazons that stood before him had brought the war to an end. He was impressed with their efforts, but he still nursed displeasure over the way they had treated him when they had been looking for information only a few moons ago.

"We need a drink," Shalmar looked to the bald old man who stared pointedly at them.

"And some food, if you have any." Jacqueline pulled up a stool beside her partner.

Nob noted that their countenance had changed considerably since the last time he saw them. They no longer looked bestial and harsh. He noticed, for a moment, that their faces showed signs of exhaustion.

He bowed slowly and departed into the back room. Shalmar turned and scanned through the sea of eyes peering at her and sighed.

"As you were," she commanded, and the rancor began again.

The folks fighting on the floor stood up and were about to resume their brawl, but the stern look Jacqueline shot their way made them think otherwise. They slowly went to a table and piped down.

The musician walked timidly back onto the stage and returned to playing his Lyre. It was a perfect blend of music and banter. The barkeeper came back shortly carrying a tray containing two steaming bowls of soup and a jug of melogion.

"On the house." Nob smiled.

The girls offered their thanks and started consuming the food. It was the first time Jacqueline had tasted food outside of Blyst. She was pleased with it. She turned to face Shalmar who was looking at her with a smile on her face.

She could see clarity in Shalmar's eyes. She seemed more relaxed, and she would like her to remain so. As she filled her stomach with the hot delicious soup, an idea crossed her mind. She turned to face the barkeeper who was tending to some new customers who had just walked in. She waited for him and gestured him over.

"So, Nob, right?" Jacqueline met his eyes curiously.

"That is the name." Nob took a dirty cloth and wiped the counter.

Shalmar was watching them intently.

"So, I hear you're quite good with information about everyone in Rheyn."

Nob wondered if the question was a new investigative tactic that the Amazons now employed. He said his next words carefully.

"I do not go looking for gossip," he grabbed a new rag from the bar. "Gossip comes naturally to me. All over this inn, what do you think they're discussing? My ears pick up the juicy details in all their conversations."

"All right," Jacqueline cut him off. She had no interest in his gossip. "Well, what do you know about Sarith?"

Bewilderment wore on Shalmar's face. She peered at Jacqueline with a quizzical stare. Jacqueline shrugged and reassured her with her eyes that she knew what she was doing. Shalmar continued to finish the hot bowl of soup and let Jacqueline press for information about her mother. All the while keeping her eyes on them both.

"You mean the woman that birthed her?" Nob pointed at Shalmar.

"Yes, what do you know about my mother?"

Nob grabbed a glass of the mead, drowned its contents swiftly, and then let out a big sigh.

"Sarith, as far as I can remember, was one of the greatest hunters of Rheyn. Blessed with the exquisite gifts by Artemis herself. She wandered in places where no hunter dared to go and slew great beasts that threatened the civility of those villages around the coast. She also displayed exceptional skills when she paddled her small vessel and her net caught fish in great numbers. She was unlike any woman I had ever known. Her bravery was much like yours. Fit for an Amazon."

He paused a moment to catch his breath. Under the glow of the lamp, the man looked weak and weary.

"Then everything changed." He looked thoughtful with his comment.

"What transpired?" Shalmar could feel her heart beating fast in her chest.

"She left for some time, didn't know if she would ever be back to Rheyn. She only came and grabbed a few things from her home, then again, she disappeared. Then we never saw or heard from her, until one day she appeared in Rheyn, her hand wrapped with yours.

"She went to another city and had me?" Shalmar raised an eyebrow to him, then glanced at Jacqueline.

"It would seem so," the old man said. "Your mother was friendly and was always in good spirits with everyone. But she always kept to herself. Her life was private. Since everyone knew how powerful she was, no one ventured to peddle false story about her disappearance for those many years and her reappearance with a girl child. Even if we all nursed curiosity, we never dared to ask. She was well respected."

Shalmar pondered on what the old man was saying. There was nothing new, apart from the fact that her mother must have conceived her in another place and had given birth to her there before coming back to Rheyn.

"Any other details about Sarith you think we should know?" Jacqueline pressed further.

Nob poured himself another glass of mead and took a swig of the cool liquid. He belched. Jacqueline winced slightly in disgust, but Shalmar's focus remained solely on Nob's words.

"Apart from the fact that she would usually roast most of her spoils before selling them off at the market, I have told you everything."

Shalmar shoulders slumped. There was not a clue she could pick up from all he disclosed to them. Jacqueline mulled his words over, and a thought creased her mind?

"Where did she roast her spoils?"

Nob paused and considered her question. "Well, not at the public abattoir, I guess. All of the hunters except her used that place."

"So, where?"

"This is rumour, and I cannot confirm it, but I heard Sarith built a hut not far from here in a meadow. Out of respect for her, nobody would dare try find it."

Shalmar's face widened in surprise. Realization struck her. If her mother had a second home, the answers to her questions could be found there.

The two women turned to each other; a smile loosely hung on Jacqueline's lips. Shalmar was already starting to stand.

They quickly raised their cups to their mouths and emptied the contents in a single simultaneous swig. As quickly as they had entered the pub, they exited, thanking Nob for his generosity and the information on their way

# CHAPTER SEVEN

Meanwhile, away from the pub, the land of Midbay splayed across the vast plains in the south. The sun had gone down, and so the day's activities were halted. The streets were deserted, even the usual drunks who roamed all the alleys had stayed behind doors this night.

At the tail end of one of the many alleys stood a magnificent bungalow. The owner, a stately built man, had gone to sleep, and the only sound that managed to pierce the stillness of the night was coming from the large shed constructed behind the house.

A smattering of pigs roamed in their stalls, the trays that were once filled with grain and soybean meal were now empty. At the end of the shed, a couple of bulls rested in their stalls. Their bodies glistened under the dull glow of the overhead lamp that hung in the centre of the shed.

Outside, a strange gust blew across the garden. As if on cue, a bright blue light flashed in front of the shed and disappeared. It was too quick for anybody who was indoors to notice, but some of the pigs in their stalls had seen the light and were startled.

The oil in the lamp was running dry, the wick burning low, and the shed was on the brink of total darkness. It was impossible for them to see the silhouette that walked in.

It had been moving from place to place after its physical body had been banished from Earth. Filled with revenge, it had tried to wake up its human body but realized that it had dissipated to ash. It was impossible for it to plan its revenge with not a host in sight.

Thankfully, a fragment of its power remained. It was not enough for it to carry out its heinous plans; it had tried to experiment its power on humans and had soon regretted it. Whenever he tried to send a blast of its power towards the humans who couldn't see him, it would backfire and strike its non-existent body.

In its fit of fury, it had tried to possess the wildest of beasts but realized that their willpower was far stronger than it had thought them to be. They expelled it out of their body as quickly as it had tried to possess them.

For every time it had tried to possess a creature and met non-acceptance, it noticed that a piece of its power disappeared. It feared the worst. But the revenge it was planning motivated it even more.

It floated into the shed, and as soon as the pigs spotted it, they oinked and squealed louder. Their noise woke the owner of the house, but the long walk from the house to the shed discouraged him from leaving the comforts of the fur that draped over his body.

The silhouette glided gently through the uproar of the shed towards the end where the bulls had just woken up.

Just as the bulls began to fuss, the silhouette yawed right into one of the stalls and possessed one of the bulls. It was a struggle that lasted for two minutes. Soon after, the bull's eyes glowed red in fury and its pointy horns glowed in the darkness.

The mage Declavius had gained the upper hand.

***

The noise from the shed grew louder every passing second. The owner of the shed couldn't risk his neighbours reporting him to the town sheriff. They were vile people, and even though he was a nobleman, they would stop at nothing to fine him for the disturbance, which would usually consist of handing away his precious livestock.

He stumbled out of the fur, slipped his legs into his boots, and grabbed the keys to the shed. He moved towards the adjacent room, lit another lamp, and walked out of the house. Wind brushed his robe as he moved hurriedly towards the direction of the shed. The noise had grown louder, and he wondered whether a foul beast had found its way onto his property. He retraced his steps in the house and went searching for a weapon. He found a blade after rummaging through the storeroom, so he grabbed the small weapon and stumbled back out into the night air.

The shed, he noticed, was still locked from the outside as he had left it earlier. As he walked closer to the shed, the noise from the animals filled his ears. He had looked after these animals all his life and he had never heard any of them make such a sound; he knew that they must be terrified.

He quickly unlocked the door and flung it open. The pigs were the first to spot him and their squeals grew even brasher. Startled, he walked to the centre of the room and looked around the shed. Swinging his bright lamp around, bewilderment crossed his face.

The pigs were scurrying mindlessly inside their stalls, searching for an exit. *But from whom,* he mused. As he approached the end of the shed, his ears picked up a strange guttural sound. At first, he thought it was a wild beast, probably a coyote, that had somehow broken into the shed. He quickly shoved the thought aside. The walls of the property had been built with the finest of materials, and it was impossible for any creature—man or beast—to encroach. The locks on the door were in perfect condition, and he was once again assured that his livestock was not being attacked by thieves or coyotes. He walked to the end to the stalls where the bulls were and checked each of them, one after the other. Apart from the fact that they were all agitated, they looked perfectly fine. The last stall was open, and he checked it to see if the bull was there.

He heaved a sigh of relief when he spotted the quiet bull. Then he heard the strange sound again, this time from the stall he was standing in front of. A gasp escaped his lips as he brought the lamp closer to the stall. The bull threw its head back, and for the first time he saw its eyes.

He took a step back in quiet disbelief and, as if on cue, the other animals in the shed started squealing more. It was a disorienting sound, and it seemed to travel far off the property.

The bull's eyes were glowing scorching red. His eyes travelled to the horns that sat on the bull's head and he realized how sharp the tips had become. They glinted in the light. The bull growled, stomping its hoof on the ground.

He stumbled out of the stall and ran frantically out of the shed. Once he was outside, he paused to catch his breath and turned around.

From a distance, he could still see the eyes of the bull glowing in fury. Without warning, it started charging towards him. Before he could gather himself to run, the bull slammed into him with such ferocity that it made his bones crack. The bull's sharp horns pierced through the robe and into his skin.

Grunting, the bull flung the man into the air and rammed into him as his body descended to the ground. The man grew still.

The noise inside the shed had started to settle down. The animals were still unnerved inside their stalls, and their eyes affixed to the entrance where the bull stood over their owner. Suddenly, the whole bull began to glow and let out a bellow before it crumpled to the ground. The light disappeared.

Declavius had left it.

An hour later, at sunrise, his wife and young son would search for him inside the house, and would eventually find him outdoors, all his life force gone. They would find a dead bull on the shale, its eyes glazed over. They would think that he had put up a brave fight against this mad bull. Both would be completely unaware of the menacing tyrant that had magically appeared and was now on the hunt for his next host.

# CHAPTER EIGHT

Her mother's hut was not far from Rheyn according to Nob. The black horses galloped into the night as the Amazons commanded them to move. They had rested enough for this short ride to the outskirts of Rheyn.

Any evidence of daylight had been replaced with the night sky. The moon shone brightly overhead and the trees cast their sinewy shadows on the main path that the horses galloped on. The air was mildly stirring with the noise of crickets chirping from every corner of the forest as they rode. As the horses swerved to the right—the hooves pounding on the loamy earth sounded like heavy thunder that filled their ears.

Shalmar was in good spirits; she was elated that they had made the decision to go to the pub instead of journeying back to the capital. She was thankful that her partner persisted to join with her against her better judgement. It was a wonderful feeling knowing that someone was sacrificing pleasures of sleep to be by her side.

Similarly, Jacqueline was somewhat spirited that the moment seemed akin to the mission they had accomplished days ago. Ever since they returned, she had longed for a mission to take her away from Blyst and fight by Shalmar's side. Even though looking for Shalmar's mother's secret hut was unlike missions Amazons were used to, it still felt gratifying.

It was no longer an issue to prove herself to her partner. She could see in the little gestures Shalmar showed her that she was impressed with her developments thus far. She smiled to herself as she thought of how far she had come in a short time.

Nob had told them the direction to follow, using his knife to draw a scraggly map on the table, before they stormed off.

As Shalmar rode, she hoped that she would find the answers she sought at this mysterious hut. Knowing her mother, it would be easy to go to and from, so it wouldn't be far out. The vision from the previous night still lingered in her mind as the horse pressed forward. She replayed it in her head, and she charged the horse some more.

Just as they began to approach another clearing in the distance, something caught her attention. She pulled on the reins skillfully, bringing the creature to a halt.

"I saw a path back there." Shalmar watched the younger warrior edge forward, curiosity on her face. "I think we should trace it out. After what Nob said, I can't see it being much further on than this. Mother would have been sensible to keep it close enough that it could be returned to with ease."

They dismounted, recited the line of the path, and steered down it slowly.

Shalmar spotted another path veering off from the one they were on. Given the circumstances, it was not easily visible for common eyes. With the intense training from a young age with her mother along with her Amazon training, Shalmar was highly skilled in following weak trails and bush paths. The brightness of the moon had made it easier.

The path Shalmar had spotted was overgrown with bushes but underneath it was a track that led lazily into the copse. She signaled Jacqueline over to the spot.

"This is the trail." Jacqueline was smiling.

They meandered on the new path, Shalmar in front, shifting the overgrown bushes with her sword, with Jacqueline and the horses following closely behind. Shalmar stopped now and then to get a feel for the direction she needed to go. She had veered off the path, but the glow of the moon helped them to retrace their steps and get back on course to the weak trail.

The path began to widen and clear out. Delighted, the warriors trudged on. The path was now void of overgrown grasses.

Shalmar slowly scanned the terrain. Her eyes strained in the darkness as she could see evidence of a small building. As they moved closer, she saw it had already been worn out with age and lack of use. Some of the timber had fallen away from the joints.

A strange feeling washed over her as she stared at the shed. She couldn't figure out why, but it all felt so familiar.

"I have been to this place before,"

She advanced into the clearing; Shalmar felt an invisible energy that was directing her. She knew this was the place where her mother built her hut so many years ago.

It was only seconds before the hut came into view. As they stood in front of it, the hut sat unfazed overlooking a small lake, which was gleaming under the moonlight. Half of it was built into a hill, making it difficult for anyone to see. The air filled their nostrils with the sweet smell of grass and honey as they proceeded towards the hut. Shalmar felt it strange but comforting.

Jacqueline walked quietly beside her. Shalmar's last statement piqued her. If she had claimed she had once been here, why did she not remember it.

Shalmar's mind was a maze of thoughts overlapping themselves. The longer she looked at the hut, the more certain she was that she had once roamed in this place before. She could already picture how it looked under a sunny sky. Whenever she tried to latch on a memory, she felt an invisible force pulling her further away.

"Shall we?" Jacqueline had situated the horses in a small area off the hut and returned to her side.

She heard her partner's voice behind her and came back to the present.

"We shall."

Shalmar proceeded to try the door. The knob let out an eerie metallic sound, which carried up into the air, the door didn't move. She turned the knob again, exerting enough strength to open it, but the disappointment registered on her face when once again the door remained firm in its hinges. The moon was shining directly on the door, giving them a slight amount of light. Shalmar realized the key she held in her poach for so many years, that she never found a home for, was likely the one for this door. The key was of an intricate design, made only by the finest blacksmith of Rheyn. She had sat and pondered its importance many times. She quickly fished through her leather pouch slung over her shoulder.

"I have always wondered what lock this particular key would fit into." Shalmar rested her thumb over an oddly shaped key on her ring of keys. The only way she could decipher the key was to feel for it as the moon was disappearing behind the hills. "My mother refused to tell me what it unlocked." She slid the key into the chamber and twisted it. They heard a small rustle and a click.

"We are here," the door creaked as it slowly parted to reveal the dark room. A torrent of wind rustled out of the room and washed over their faces. The warriors looked curiously at each other. Both sensed the meaning behind the wind but were not able to put words to it.

The moons rays were dimmer now, the light it offered was not enough for them to weave their way around the hut. Jacqueline spotted a small lamp slumbering in the corner and grabbed it. There was still some oil inside it. As Jacqueline lit the lamp, the room came alive as the light danced throughout. Both women took a moment to take everything in. The space was welcoming and had a warmth to it. A sense of love passed through Shalmar. She watched as her partners eyes met hers, and Jacqueline nodded in understanding, as she too was touched by the feeling as well.

The hut was more spacious than they had expected. Two wooden chairs were neatly arranged on the right with a small table positioned in front of them. Shalmar spotted spears leaning on the wall, casting long shadows on the ground. There was also a fishing net hung on a nail that had been punctured into the wall. A couple of plates, covered with dust, were neatly stacked with some pots on the counter.

With every step, Shalmar gazed around the room. She quickly came to the realization that this place wasn't just a haven where her mother kept her hunting gear. It began to look more like Sarith had settled here for a time before returning to live the rest of her days in Rheyn. It was a home.

She noticed some scratchy writings and drawings etched into the clay and mud walls, and she moved closer to inspect them. It didn't make much sense to her as her eyes roved over every detail. There were lines and circles in all kinds of patterns, she mused. It could've only been written by a... *These were made by a child*, she thought.

The thought disappeared as quickly as it had formed. Shalmar shook her head, her heart racing. She realized that she was close to the answer, even more than she had expected to be.

Jacqueline's voice broke through the silence. "There is another room."

Shalmar turned to face her partner and followed her eyes. As soon as her eyes connected with the door of the adjacent room, she heard a voice in her head.

*Come.*

Shalmar blinked and saw Jacqueline waiting for her. Shalmar advanced to the door, her arm outstretched to twist the knob. Shock registered on her face when the door slid open before her hand made contact.

Tensed, she slowly entered the room. Jacqueline followed shortly with the lamp in one hand, and the fingers of her other hand gingerly caressing the hilt of a small blade on her waist. She wasn't going to let her guard down. Even though the place seemed safe it was still strange territory to her.

The room was cozy, as though a significant amount of the northern air was trapped inside. There were no windows, they realized quickly. A large fur rug was draped on the ground on the right side.

It was all starting to come back to her. Lost memories trapped in the bottom of her mind began to rise to the surface. Shalmar could feel her internal senses widening as she took in every detail. The wooden walls. The fur rugs. The pile of old clothes.

On pure instinct, she proceeded to the left side of the room where a small wooden bed sat with a fur draped on it. At the head of the fur sat two pillows woven from wool. As she reached out and casually touched a pillow, a shift occurred in the room.

A massive sphere of deep purple light flashed in the room, engulfed Shalmar, and began to lift her off the ground. She couldn't control the energy that was all around her. The energy had become her, and she it.

Her eyes closed.

Jacqueline reached out to unsheathe her sword. She wasn't sure what she was supposed to battle against—what was that unseen force controlling Shalmar?

"Shalmar," she screamed as the light began to elevate her partner higher into the air. Shalmar's eyes were closed, and her arms were stiff and outstretched. She hung motionless in the air.

For the first time in a long time, Jacqueline felt helpless. She didn't know how to approach the situation before her. Her feet were planted firmly on ground as she raised her sword, which seemed to jitter every passing second.

"Shalmar."

Shalmar could hear Jacqueline's voice in a distance. She was in stasis. Floating in a massive void like the one in her dream. The void transformed into a reality of another sort. A memory that had been locked away for so long played before her eyes. It was an out-of-body experience; she was outside looking in.

She was standing outside the hut. A clear bright sky above, the meadow vibrant and alive with colour. As she marvelled at the beauty that surrounded her, the door creaked open and two small girls poured out and began to race towards the shore of the lake.

One of them looked familiar; the girl, not more than five years old, was leading the smaller girl. Shalmar made a rough guess and placed her age at three.

"Shalmar," she heard a voice calling out from inside. It registered in her head. It was unmistakably her mother. "Watch after your sister."

Shalmar blinked at the statement as it caught her off guard. She stole a quick glance at the kids who were now playing beside the lake. With a jolt, she realized that the child with the chestnut braided hair, the child with the grey green eyes, the child who was seemingly taller and bigger than the other was her.

It was surreal, the moment. Seeing her younger self.

When she turned to face the door, Sarith was standing there, arms akimbo, watching the girls play in the distance. She looked confident and powerful, yet she held a warm composure.

Her dark hair fell freely by her side, dancing lightly as the breeze caressed it. She was young, her face free of the wrinkles that come with age.

If there was something that Shalmar noted more than anything else that surprised her, it was the mere fact that her mother was happy here. She was smiling as she watched the energetic girls play not far from the hut.

"Mother?" Shalmar spoke softly. She soon realized that it was futile as her mother stood there unfazed. She waved her hands at her mother, but Sarith never looked at her. It was as though she was not there.

"Let the girls play. They will be alright."

Shalmar heard a distant voice, emanating from inside the hut. The voice belonged to her father.

"Come inside."

Shalmar watched as her mother smiled and retreated inside the home, leaving the door ajar. Shalmar turned to face the girls. They were no longer screaming gleefully, she noticed. They were sitting on the log on the shore and giggling quietly.

Shalmar never knew she had a young sister. She had no memory of this scene. As she watched the young girls, a minor disruption of the grass beside them caught her attention. She gasped in horror when something appeared from the lawn. It was a brown serpent; lean and long, and it slithered towards the unsuspecting girls. Seeing this, Shalmar willed her body forward to protect them. Her form remained rooted to the spot.

The reality of it all struck her; this was a memory and her action or inaction would not change the fate of what happened. She could only watch. The serpent had already crawled to striking distance, its lean mouth widening and poised to attack the younger child.

"Shalmar." She found herself screaming to her younger self.

Just as the creature lunged at them, the chestnut-haired girl dragged the smaller child to her chest.

They watched the creature sail over the space where the younger girl once sat.

"Fernella, stay behind me."

Shalmar heard her younger self screaming instructions to her sister. *Fernella.* That was her sister's name. Warmth filled her as the child ran and took position behind her. It would seem the serpent wasn't satisfied with its defeat. It recoiled, and its menacing head turned to them.

Shalmar watched as her younger self slowly bent down and grabbed a small rock from the ground.

"No one hurts my sister." She heard her scream.

With a blinding fury, she hurled the stone towards the snake. It made an arc in the air, gathering momentum, and crashed right into the space between its eyes. Shalmar, watching from a distance, marveled how her aim could be that accurate.

Shalmar could swear that kind of accuracy could only be honed after many years of training. Even with rigorous training, some Amazons found it difficult to pull that off.

The snake's head was skewed off to a rather eccentric angle, and crimson oozed out of a large gash that had been cut open by the rock. Like a drunk, its head swaggered sideways, and it fell to the ground, the life it once had was no longer.

"Let's go back inside," the younger Shalmar said to the other child. She held her hand and led her to the home.

Shalmar beamed with joy as she watched the retreating figures. She was very pleased that she had handled herself well even as a child. As she stood there, the bright clear day gave way to darkness. She was still outside the hut, but the season had changed. It was spring and she could feel her body being pulled towards the house.

As her body glided into the hut, she saw her mother standing at the corner; sadness like a second skin was evident on her face. A single lamp was glowing in the center of the room—exactly where Jacqueline had found the lamp just moments ago.

A man draped with a white robe was standing beside Sarith. She didn't need an introduction. This man was her father.

The upper part of his body was draped with a cloak patterned with the finest designs. In all her life, Shalmar had never seen any cloak this beautiful before. She saw his eyes and a gasp escaped her lips. They were grey-green, just like hers. He had a wide oval face hidden inside the cloak. With a jounce, she realized that the man standing beside her mother was the same man who had appeared in her dream the previous night, riding the white horse.

He was the man who had sent her on this course that had revealed a past that had been buried for so long.

"We agree. Shalmar will remain with you, while I take Fernella to Jadehollow." She heard him say. "With Shalmar here, Fernella will one day become ruler of the Air Element, taking my place at the throne."

While the statement seemed odd to her, the man left her mother and walked into the adjoining room. Suddenly, Shalmar could feel her body gliding after him.

He carried a lamp with him to the room, filling the space with a soft glow as he navigated to the small fur rug. Her younger self and her sister, Fernella, were soundly floating in unconsciousness.

He knelt beside her younger self. She had never seen so much sorrow on one person before. Even her mother, on her worst days, did not come close to the sorrow her father clearly felt.

Suddenly, she started to hear a strange chant emanating from him. He was chanting in a language that she had never heard before. As he continued to chant, a dark purple light appeared on his fingertips, an energy she hadn't seen before. She watched it flow all over his body and settle on his forehead. He opened his eyes; they were no longer green but a whitish purple.

He moved his fingers to touch her forehead and she could see the energy being transported from father to child. It made her younger self jerk, but she never woke up.

Slowly, after the process had been completed, her father bent his head and kissed her forehead.

"Goodbye, Shalmar," her father said, close to tears. "Maybe one day you'll understand the implications of what just happened tonight. Maybe one day you'll forgive my actions and open your eyes to see the bigger picture."

Shalmar was moved to tears. All the resentment, all the pain she had stored for the father she never knew, was dissolving from her. She now knew that he wasn't a coward or a destitute. He was a man who loved his children and his family.

She watched him rise to his feet and move to the side of the rug where Fernella was. Slowly, he hefted her into his arms and walked out of the room.

****

Jacqueline was worried. She had never seen such magic that held her partner. Shalmar was floating in mid-air, her eyes closed and her body stiff, sharp energy all around her.

Jacqueline's sword was still raised in the air, sangfroid, waiting for any hint, any indication of an imminent attack. Even though what was unfolding confused her, her defiance and bravery was evidenced in the way she stood before the floating body.

Her mind was running several possible scenarios. Who would want to hurt Shalmar? The problem with that question was even though the Amazons were respected and feared in some parts, they managed to amass a lot of enemies along the way.

After running through a bunch of lowlifes and petty thieves in her mind, she shrugged. None of them could wield the kind of resolve to conjure up a magic that would keep her in place like this.

As she pondered the strangeness of the situation that befell them, a bright white light flashed across the room. Shalmar's body descended to the floor. She opened her eyes; her green pupils had been replaced with a glowing white light, which now seemed to flow all over her body.

Suddenly, the light pulled back inside of her and she landed gently on her feet.

"Shalmar?"

Jacqueline sheathed her sword in her scabbard and rushed to her side. The older warrior blinked, briefly checking her surroundings. On spotting Jacqueline, she pulled her into a warm embrace.

"What happened?" Jacqueline's eyes searched her face.

"I was taken to my past," Shalmar touched her cheek. "I cannot fully explain the magic that made it happen, but I understand everything now." She disengaged herself slowly and kissed Jacqueline's lips.

It was then she felt it. The untapped energy welling inside her; the powers surging to be brought to the surface.

Shalmar shifted away. She felt a powerful energy flowing from her hands. Jacqueline followed as Shalmar went out of the small house. Shalmar couldn't contain the energy that was threatening to explode through her palms. She focused her attention on a large broken tree, a mass of cold bristling air shot out her hands and she elevated the broken half of the tree into the air. She laid it across the pathway, making the entrance to this place even more difficult to find.

Jacqueline could not believe what was happening. Everything was lit up and immersed with energy. She knew there was no need to be afraid of Shalmar, but she wasn't sure of what she was witnessing and how it was all coming about.

"I hope you are willing to let me explain," Shalmar turned to face Jacqueline. She could feel her partner's apprehension.

Shalmar's voice was soft as she looked to her partner with love in her eyes. She knew this may be too much for Jacqueline to understand. Jacqueline, searching Shalmar's green eyes, inhaled deeply. She offered her hand to Shalmar and they returned indoors. After a brief conversation, as sleep called to them, the warriors settled in the hut and welcomed rest. They had decided they would ride back to Blyst in the morning.

# CHAPTER NINE

"A day will come when your reign will end. One who joins the world will defeat you. She is one of the three that has been spoken of since the dawn of time. The change is coming, and your end will be swift, Greenflack. Turn to the Fragahns at your peril. They are more than your fragile mind can control. You will rue this day, the day you become the ruler of Jadehollow, for it is not your destiny. You dare to defy fate and you will pay the price with your very soul"

With a wave of his hand, Greenfleck shut the words out of his head. It had been getting annoyingly incessant the last few days. He knew it was the Dolchie. He had heard these words in his mind since he had killed the Dolchie and relinquished its power.

An insect had been hovering around his head like a bad omen. With a devilish grin on his face, he snapped his fingers. Instantly, a fireball appeared and engulfed the insect, leaving no room for escape. The heat turned it to ash immediately. He snapped his fingers again and the fire disappeared.

In hindsight, he was glad to have silenced the blasted oracle himself. It was a risk he was willing to bear. He couldn't have imagined Em wielding the powers that he now held. At first it was difficult to control the magic swirling inside him, threatening to break his resolve.

It was a disgrace to take the life of a Dolchie and the repercussions were dire. Or so he was told. Right now, he felt that he had kept it under control quite well. Over the last three days, he had been experimenting with his new powers.

A burnt acre of land later, he knew he was coming to terms with the power that was in him. The power that now *was* him. His evil machinations began to fuel it until the point he was sure that he could handle himself.

After the Princess Fernella escaped his hand, he had sent Em and a couple of scouts after her. Three nights have passed, and he hadn't gotten word of their progress or failure. It was unlike Em to have not returned.

It could only mean one of two things, Greenflack rose to his feet. Something unfortunate had happened to Em and the scouts as they went after Fernella, who ran away with the King of the Passers or they had decided to display cowardice and deviated from their mission.

Either way, it was in his hands to make it right. He already rounded up the last of the Passers who had survived the bloodbath when he was fighting to take over the city. Six of them. He had kept them locked away in a makeshift prison along with the natives of Jadehollow, torturing them day and night.

Even though their screams had somewhat quenched his thirst, it was not enough to suppress the hunger that welled up inside him.

He wanted Fernella to be his primary mate—no matter the cost. If she did not succumb to his wishes, he would end her life along with her stepmother's, and begin his reign as supreme leader of Jadehollow.

Since his men had failed him, he began to devise another plan. He was convinced beyond reasonable doubt that Fernella had escaped with the King of the Passers to Turonia, the city of the Water Element.

He had never been there; he had only heard stories of how the Water and Air people once lived in the same lands, before they parted to build their own kingdoms. He wasn't clear on the rivalry between the two cities or if there even was one.

If Fernella, the future Queen of the Air Element, was welcomed with open arms, he mused, then the rivalry was non-existent. He would have to launch an attack on them. With Em gone with half of his soldiers, the odds of gaining the upper hand on a surprise attack were slim.

He would need assistance of some sort.

*The Fragahns.* An evil grin spread across his lips. As he wiped the specks of dust from his robe, he heard the words of the Dolchie in his head.

*Turn to the Fragahns at your peril. They are more than your fragile mind can control.*

He laughed. With the kind of power, he now held, his destiny was in his hands. It was not going to be any other way.

"I will bend the Fragahns to my will, whether they succumb to my wishes or not."

And with that, he began to venture deep into the forest, moving south.

# CHAPTER TEN

It was mid-morning when they set out of the small shack in the meadow. The sun was slowly peeking out of the clouds like a shy lover, and the scent of wildflowers filled the air as they began a slow saunter to the lake.

It had been an interesting night. Jacqueline had listened to Shalmar talk about her experience and loved that she openly answered the questions Jacqueline put forth. The conversation had been short as the exhaustion from the day's events had caught up with them. It was surprising to know that memories from her childhood had been locked up in her mind.

Talking about her childhood was surreal and overwhelming for Shalmar. She understood the vision and what it all meant. Her sister, Fernella, who had disappeared with her father, the King of Jadehollow, was in apparent danger. From the memory she saw when she was in stasis, she could only think her parents did it to honour the destiny the girls both had and to protect them from harm. If one found out they were connected to his lineage, it could make them both targets. From the discussions she overhead her parents have, she had been fated to be an Amazon warrior—it was nice to know that she had fulfilled her destiny. If Fernella had been fated to be ruler over the land of Jadehollow, and she was in danger, the throne is threatened.

Then came the issue of her powers. Jacqueline had been befuddled about how Shalmar could transmit an energy—which seemed to manipulate the air to do her bidding—out of her hands. Jacqueline saw that Shalmar could suspend objects in the air. She wondered what else her partner could do as she mastered her new talent. Concerned plagued her mind. She had seen what powers could do with the experience they had with the mage. They had barely escaped the attack of the mage, Declavius, who had magically appeared in the palace of King Yarael. Seeing Shalmar possess such powers frightened her. It was not Shalmar she doubted; it was the magic she held. She had grown quiet and knew that her partner would notice the change in her.

"I sense you are unsure of all this?" Shalmar touched Jacqueline's arm and for a moment they stood still. She studied Shalmar's face thoughtfully.

"I am unsure of it, yes. I have gone from hearing about magic in stories told, to fighting with a mage, to this." Jacqueline, now moving again, always felt better if she was walking while discussing things. She never understood why, but she preferred it. Shalmar glanced over at her as they were both lost in thought.

"I understand it is different. I understand if you are afraid or unsure. Just know that I would not hurt you."

"I know this to be true. I just have no idea how this... magic works."

They had met the lake shore and Shalmar turned to face her.

"This is new for me as well, Jacqueline. I have no choice but to accept it and learn it. If it frightens you and you want to end your part of the journey and return home, I will respect that."

Jacqueline searched the depths of Shalmar's green eyes. Shalmar silently removed her garments and went to refresh herself in the lake.

Jacqueline took in her partners svelte body as she disappeared in the water. She knew she did not want to return home.

Shalmar could feel the intensity of the energy moving within her from this power she now possessed. She hoped with more practice she could take this urgent fire that was becoming a part of her and master it with ease. She heard the water behind her and knew Jacqueline had decided to stay. Watching Jacqueline bathe and slowly emerge with beads of water rolling down her tight supple skin, Shalmar smiled slowly. She decided what she should do with the vivacity she was feeling.

As Jacqueline passed by her, Shalmar reached out and drew her body into hers. Their eyes held in a long transparent gaze. Shalmar could feel the mixture of emotions that passed through her lover since the discovery of her powers. There was nothing more Shalmar wanted than to reassure Jacqueline, and herself, there was nothing to fear.

Shalmar's mouth brushed hypnotically across Jacqueline's. Jacqueline arched her head back, shuttering as Shalmar's lips left a warm trail to the tender part of her neck. She felt herself tremble to her core as Shalmar's teeth bit her skin in that perfect way. Her head spinning as her nails dug into her lover's arms to brace herself. As Shalmar's fingertips slid over her back, Jacqueline felt the intensity within her surge. Shalmar placed her hands over Jacqueline's hips, lifting her as she wrapped her slender thighs around Shalmar's waist. Their eyes collided; their lips met in a deep, haunting kiss. Shalmar moved them easily from the water. She lay Jacqueline down in the willowy green grass amongst the brilliance of the flowers and did what she intended to do. As the sun kissed their skin with its warmth and vigour, Shalmar moved the intense energy that was fuelling her into her partner. Every part of Jacqueline's being was ignited as Shalmar's mouth and hands found their way to the most sensitive, vulnerable parts of her. As her cries of satisfaction echoed throughout the morning air, a radiant sphere of deep purple light enveloped them. Jacqueline, with an ache to have Shalmar closer, pulled Shalmar on top of her. Their bodies pressing together, moving fluently in unison. When their eyes held, they could feel their essence merge and ripple through each other in infinite ways. Their consciousness connected at a frequency so powerful it was met with a brilliant burst of colours and, without knowing it, in their surrender, Shalmar had consummated with her primary mate.

They lay in each other's arms, still marvelling at the new level of rapture they had shared. The sun shifted in the sky and Shalmar knew it was time to start their journey. They dressed, and in silence, they locked up the hut and gathered the horses. As Jacqueline reached for her horse, Shalmar placed her hand on her forearm. Their gaze held as they searched each other's eyes. They could feel the shift; they could feel the depth of the connection between them in an unexplainable way. Shalmar took Jacqueline's face delicately in her hands.

"Jacqueline, I love you. May the goddess Aphrodite know these words I speak to be true on this day."

Jacqueline could feel tears stream down her cheeks as Shalmar wiped them away. She had never known these feelings before.

"I have loved you far beyond the present day, Shalmar. This I knew when I first saw you. The music of the muses etched a song in my heart today that I will hold for no other than you."

They held each other, then foreheads touching, they kissed and moved to continue their journey to Blyst.

The horses galloped easily on the path. Shalmar's senses were heightened. She could hear a couple of squirrels squabbling for nuts, though they were a significant distance away. She could feel and see everything around her more detailed, more focused.

She was now one with the environment. She could hear them, and they could hear her. She realized that her powers not only flowed through her hands, they were also telepathic.

She had wished that the thicket would clear off while the horse trudged on the path, and she gasped when the leaves started swaying sideways, creating a clear trail for them to cross. Jacqueline, riding behind her, was flummoxed, but maintained a calm demeanour as she noted the way nature was responding to her partner. She was not frightened of Shalmar in any way. She was still trying to absorb all that had happened. The closeness they had just shared was helping her transition with the knowing and accepting of it. She knew, as unsure of magic as she was, she was sure of Shalmar and her feelings for her.

With time, Shalmar realized that she was starting to feel drained. It was the consequences of exerting so much energy around her and not quite understanding how to balance it. The journey back to Blyst was a lengthy one, so it would require a quick stop over at Rheyn to fill their stomachs with food. She needed to conserve her strength.

She inhaled deeply, shutting off the energy inside her core. She knew she had much to learn of this.

"You must journey through the Western Sea to the Numinous Sea," Shalmar's voice breaking the silence. "Find the edge of the continent, only then shall you find what was long taken from you."

"Those were his exact words?" Jacqueline was riding beside her.

"Yes. I have replayed it in my head since I heard them in my dream."

They got to the main path that led to Rheyn and picked up their pace.

"Now I know what was taken from me," Shalmar cocked an eyebrow. "My sister, Fernella."

"And from what he said, we need to find her at the edge of the continent, which is through the Western Sea and the Numinous Sea." Jacqueline directed her horse over a mud hole and realigned beside Shalmar.

"We'll need some maps. The map that shows all the land and seas around the continent."

"Where can we find such maps?"

"That's the problem. There's only one place in the whole of Gilsk that has what we are seeking. Command Tower."

"We don't have the clearance to be permitted access to the vaults of those quarters," Jacqueline noted. "Even the school instructors do not have such access. It can only be authorized by a member of the Supreme Order."

Shalmar thought about the meeting she had with Sym. Sym wasn't pleased with her response—declining the offer of becoming a hallowed member of the Supreme Order.

Sym would need some convincing of some sort.

"I'll think of something to tell Sym."

The sun had come out in its full glory, beaming down on them. The outskirt of Rheyn was beginning to come into view when Jacqueline remembered something from the vision Shalmar had disclosed.

"Even if we manage to get our hands on the maps," she spoke over the loud thunder of hooves. "One crucial part of the mission is left to be established."

"Which is?"

"A boat to sail through those seas." Jacqueline raised her eyebrow as she had someone in mind. "Someone who knows these waters and can meander us safely in the face of enemy attack. Most importantly, someone we can share your secrets with."

Shalmar smiled. She was proud of the young woman whose mind was as alert and as skilled as her instincts.

"I like that you think like this," Shalmar, commanding the horse away from the main road to Rheyn, changing course. "Let's check up on our mutual acquaintance, shall we?"

***

"Get that thief. Help me. Get that thief."

The scream of a helpless trader woke her up. A few seconds passed and she heard a pattering of footsteps that seemed to lapse into silence. She flung herself out of the bed and stumbled to the door.

The shoreline of Midbay spread out before her eyes. The fishermen were carrying out the monotonous ritual of washing their nets, their faces serious and brooding. Her eyes roved wildly, until she spotted a middle-aged woman raising her hands in frustration and screaming obscenities.

Darting through the scanty mass of people, was a man with a basket of goods nestled in his arms. The townsfolk moved on with their business, not bothering to apprehend the stone-faced youth carting away with stolen goods.

She gritted her teeth.

One second, she was back in her room, the next she was out with a quiver slung over her shoulder and her bow deftly grasped in her left hand. The thief had just cut and yawed through an alley, an alley she was very familiar with from her travels.

Settling herself, she took a long slow drag of air and took chase. A couple of pigeons fluttered away from the ground, making a path for her as she pursued the thief.

He was fast, but the huntress was faster. She soon zoomed past the woman who had begun to think her basket was lost. When the woman spotted Noieh, she recognized her from town. As Noieh was racing towards the thief, the woman threw her hands up in jubilation.

A couple of seconds later, the huntress sped into the alley the thief had entered. Noieh paused to catch her breath. She spotted him in the distance, running wildly between the few people that had taken residence there.

Noieh considered her options: if she used an arrow, aimed and slung it, the chance of missing the target with all the debris around and hitting an innocent was possible. She decided it would be easier to close the distance between them, allowing her a decent shot.

She took off again, the thumping of her feet matching the thumps of her heart. She would not let this swine get away.

The thief realized that someone was tailing him. With a grunt, he increased his pace and swerved into another lane way.

Thankfully, there was no one milling around. It afforded him the opportunity to displace the woman behind him once and for all. His feet thudded on the earth as his body moved. His strength was waning, but he kept on running.

He ran to the end of the street and turned. She was still far off, bounding down the deserted street towards him. He stole a quick glance at the basket he had stolen and contemplated ditching it.

No, he wouldn't.

He jetted off in another direction. It was still deserted; he could see the next street in the distance. A sea of townsfolk was flowing at the junction. If he could get there unhurt, he would mingle with the mass and disappear.

As if reading his thoughts, Noieh came to a halt. Her hand flew to the quiver behind her and grabbed an arrow. Slowly, she affixed the arrow on the string and raised it to her shoulder.

In between breaths, she released her bow. The arrow darted through the air, speeding towards its target.

As the thief took another step, the arrow buried itself in the ankle of his right leg. The pain was sharp and numbing. It pummelled him to the ground, his grip on the basket loosened.

The basket spilled over; balls of fruit scattered extensively. Those townsfolk who noticed him moved on mindlessly without a second glance. That was the way of the people of Midbay.

He tried to scramble to his feet, but it was difficult. He turned and saw the arrow sticking out of his leg, he groaned in pain. Removing the arrow would be suicide if he couldn't stop the bleeding.

He didn't care about recovering the fruit that had spilled over. There was only one thing on his mind now—escape. Grumbling, he struggled to stand up. As he attempted to hop to safety, he felt another searing pain on his left ankle. Howling, he crumpled to the ground yet again. Another arrow had stuck his other leg.

Seeing that her arrows had done the minimal damage she intended, she approached him, a grim grin on her face. He tried to crawl away from her, the attempt was useless. There was no way he would get far.

"Well, well, well. What do we have here?" He heard the sarcastic remark behind him. "A petty thief, aren't you?"

"You bitch," he cursed as he struggled to get up on his feet.

Before he could stand up, her foot connected with his head, sending his face to make unsolicited romance with the ground. As she went to grab him, a neigh sound broke through the silence of the alley. She glanced up and saw two black geldings with Amazon warriors jumping down in unison. The sight was impressive.

"You might want to save your energy, Noieh," They were smiling. "We got a little proposition for you."

She grinned. She knew who they were. She had, in fact, helped them on a mission a few moons ago. She rushed forward towards them and bowed her head.

The thief, seeing his only opportunity to escape with the timely distraction, began to crawl to the wall.

The younger of the Amazons had spotted him and calmly approached him.

"Someone needs to teach you that you shouldn't utter such loathsome words to a lady."

And with that, she brought her boot down to his face, sending him into unconsciousness. The kick wasn't enough to send him to his grave—it was just enough to make him reconsider his line of business when he eventually came to. Shalmar and Noieh exchanged a chuckle as they watched Jacqueline tend to the thief.

They saw a woman bounding down the streets towards them. It was the woman that had her goods stolen. Without even muttering thanks to Noieh, the woman quickly gathered her fruits and hurried away.

Shalmar was filled with bewilderment. She had never seen such display of arrogance and impudence from a villager before. These sorts of acts were usually akin to people with royal blood flowing through their veins. A notable face flashed in her mind and she disregarded it.

"Noieh, how soon can you get a boat stocked with food and supplies?" Jacqueline turned to the huntress who had nursed her back to health during their escape from those blasted Zal creatures.

"By the morrow."

"Good," Shalmar smiled. "We will leave at midday. Unless of course you have something better to do?" The two warriors cast a humorous look at their friend.

Noieh was already on the move to get her vessel. "Midday it is." She took off sporting a huge grin.

# CHAPTER ELEVEN

Beyond the vast mountain plains that bounded the towns of Kavarr, Kjell, and Orrok, situated in the south west, stood an island in the fire hills of Dargoon which had existed for eternities.

It was invisible to human eyes, for it was not a land inhabited by humans. A supernatural power created a dome that covered the vast area of the island. Adventurers in ages past had tried to locate this mystery, but the powers that protected the island would send them to deviate their course.

For over 600 years, no one had come close to finding it. Until now.

The Island of Dargoon was home of the magical creatures that once roamed the earth. Since humankind learnt how to tap into the well of magic and bended it to their wishes, the Fragahns had existed and guided them in mastering and manipulating their newfound power.

No one knew where they came from. The usual rumour passed down through the ages was that the mighty All, having seen that the pace of civilization on Earth had slowed, had sent them down to assist humans.

The Fragahns were unusual creatures. Their bodies were covered with a thick scaly skin that flowed from their neck to their long tails, almost like a protective shell. They had a humanoid face, save for their pupils, which glowed bright orange. Their mouths were parched and their teeth jagged.

They looked beastly but kept a calm composure.

They, along with other magical creatures, had yielded to the wishes of men and assisted in the progress of civilization. As more generations came to be, the hearts of men began to be corrupted beyond redemption. Greed reigned supreme. Mages no longer used their powers for the betterment of all.

Since they were commanded to obey the wishes of men, the mages ordered them to wreak havoc on others who were too weak to protect themselves. A bloody war lingered until Yarael 1st concocted a magic so potent that it helped banish the evil mages to a dreary desolate island in the north.

The same magic freed the Fragahns and the other magical beings from their submissiveness to humans, and they went on a self-imposed exile, removing themselves from civilization. Since they wanted no part in the policies of men, they set out building theirs in the Island of Dargoon.

Suffice to say, they had lived most of their lives on the Island, and they were willing to do what was needed in order to ensure it remained that way.

When they spotted a lone figure crossing the fire hills unscathed, they knew that trouble was nigh. They were sure he possessed an energy unlike the others who had once ventured dangerously into these parts.

They watched him cross a boulder and head towards the boundary line of their invisible space.

"Let him come," one of them growled. Deokyle, the oldest of them all, was their ruler. She was seated in a golden throne watching the figure with keen interest.

The island splayed out before Greenflack. It was easily the most beautiful thing he had ever seen. For a moment, he thought about coveting the land for himself. He would do so, after he bent these creatures to his will. The power that had stirred inside him, the life force of the Dolchie, had led him through to this place, and he was sure that the same power was adequate to command all the creatures of the island.

As he stepped over the boundary onto the island, he felt an uneasiness creeping up under his skin. He shrugged it aside and adjusted his gaze to the unnatural brightness of the terrain before him. He took one step and paused.

A mass of creatures with orange glowing eyes stumbled onto the path, blocking him from moving farther. He blinked and noted the aura that floated around each of them. A devilish grin extended his lips.

"Make way for him," a voice commanded in the distance.

On cue, the creatures grumbled and crawled out of the way, making a straight path to the creature that sat on a golden throne.

Greenflack covered the short distance between them. An expectant silence hung in the air as both man and creature stared into each other's eyes.

"Why have you come here?" Deokyle sat unconcerned.

"To commandeer an army," Greenflack barked, not bothered by the uneven terrain he had stepped into. The powers of the Dolchie were intoxicating. He could feel it all around him.

"I knew this day would come," Deokyle's laughter was loud. "For several hundreds of years, we have kept our island protected from the prying eyes of man. Thankfully, the mages were exiled to an island where they would spend the rest of their miserable days." The Fragahns snickered as Deokyle continued.

"Coming here was not a very bright choice. As you have probably guessed, we are under no obligations to carry out the wishes of men. Under the influence and control of men in times past, we did a lot of harm to the world, some of which still haunts us this very day. We have been freed from that hold and have adjusted to this life of solitude. We intend to maintain that life," the creature finished with finality.

"You must obey me," Greenflack gave a wave of his hand and a fireball appeared out of thin air. Grunting, he hurled the fireball towards the creature on the golden throne.

As the fire arched closer to her face, she muttered a strange word. A ball of water appeared, swallowed up the fireball, and then vanished.

"You dare come to our land and demand such things of us?" Deokyle took him by surprise. It was sudden, too sudden for Greenflack to process. The next thing he knew, he was hurtling in the air. The power that sent him flying clearly came from the Fragahn Queen and all the Fragahns of Dargoon. Their eyes all glowed, transmitting sparks to the insolent brat that had come to endanger their peace.

He tried to control his downward spiral, but soon realized it was futile. The energy that was flowing through their eyes was so powerful it overshadowed his. It was as though the power of the Dolchie was nowhere to be found.

In seconds, gravity took control, and he was falling helplessly. He yelled as he crashed on the loamy earth. A sharp searing pain shot through his whole body.

"The temerity" Deokyle raising her arms. Greenflack's body was raised off the ground with the movement, floating effortlessly. He was weak, helpless, and scared. "Let it be known that the Fragahns want no part in your civilization or destruction. This is the last time you will set foot on this island."

The creature began to utter a strange singsong. As she did, Greenflack was flung across the island beyond the boundary lines.

"Attempt to return and you will meet your death. It will be a slow, painful one at that."

His bulky body smashed to the ground. He groaned as he struggled to stand on weary feet. His strength finally returned to him, and when he looked back to the boundary lines, he realized it wasn't there anymore. The island had completely vanished.

Even with the powers of the Dolchie inside him, he could no longer see the island. He strained his eyes, hoping to find a glimpse of it, but there was nothing.

Shoulders slouched and fuelled with rage; he started the long walk back to Jadehollow.

*Turn to the Fragahns at your peril.* The Dolchie had been right after all. The prophecy now scared him. He shook his head, dismissed it from his thoughts, and allowed his rage to guide him.

He began to brew another plan.

# CHAPTER TWELVE

It was sundown when the warriors galloped into Blyst. After discussing the details of their mission, Noieh had set off energetically to get what they would need in Midbay. She would wait for them at the shore where they would journey together.

Due to the urgency of their situation to save her sister, Shalmar and Jacqueline went immediately to Sym.

It was unusual to appear at Command Tower without an official request from any member of the Supreme Order. Fortunately, Sym was in her quarters and had spotted them. She came down to receive them herself.

Shalmar had already concocted a plan—a long shot, she mused, after she had mulled it over in her mind.

Jacqueline opted to wait at the door while Shalmar followed Sym into her office. Shalmar was relieved her partner was not present as she wasn't sure how she would react to the deal Shalmar was about to put forth.

"What brings you here?" Sym returned to her chair.

"Two things." Shalmar adjusted in her seat. "I need your permission to explore the vaults." No time for niceties. Sym appreciated that in Shalmar. It was always to the point. "I need to rift through some maps."

"For that kind of permission to be granted, I need to be privy to the reasons why," Sym said as she studied the warrior before her. There was something about her physical appearance that had changed since she last saw her days prior. She couldn't pinpoint it yet. She noted the warrior was more confident, if that was even possible, as she already held herself with a self-confidence not seen in many others. She had always known her to be a strong, bold woman, but the aura she exuded in her office today was something new.

"It is of a personal matter." Shalmar locked eyes with Sym. "I promise to tender a full brief on it when I am done."

"The vaults have not been opened in years. If you were in my place, you'd understand the position you have placed me. A curiosity that needs to be satisfied."

"I cannot speak of it until I'm sure it has been completed."

"A request like this usually comes with a price," Sym's eyes boring into Shalmar's. "What's your price, Shalmar?"

Shalmar thought hard about it. It was what she guessed, and if it had to come to making a choice as difficult as this, her immediate family would come first. Her voice pierced through the air inside the office.

It was a request Sym could not refuse. Shalmar buried her feelings, but Sym saw through it all.

"Very well then. You have my permission." Sym moved to the cupboard situated at the corner. After fishing through the contents, she produced a key, which she handed to Shalmar.

"When the guard sees this, they will know I sent you. Go to the left side of the vaults. Nothing leaves the structure."

"Thank you."

"I will hold you to it, this agreement." Sym locked eyes with Shalmar, who quietly nodded and took the key.

***

The huge concrete doors of the underground vaults creaked like beasts woken from a deep slumber as Shalmar slotted the key into the keyhole. The guards stationed at the entrance handed lamps to them both.

The vault was a large storage facility that had served its purpose—safeguarding important Gilskian scrolls and treasures. It was one of the most protected buildings in all Gilsk; playing second only to the royal castle where the queen resided.

The sound of their boots hitting the marbled floor echoed down the halls. The damp air coursed into their lungs as they marched on, swinging the lamp in every direction and scanning the various sections for the one that held the maps.

It took a while before they located it. It was at the end of the hall, stacked in a glass compartment with a large dusty table positioned before it and an old magnified glass perched on it.

Smiling, they opened the compartment and poured all the parchments on the table. The first map they spread out showed a strategic view of the capital city. It was well detailed and precise; it was not the map they were looking for.

After rifling through the many parchments and scrolls, they stumbled on a map showing all the major seas in the continent. Quickly, they grabbed the viewing glass and began to examine the details.

It was a series of convoluted lines overlapping each other. They were not strangers to this sort of map presentation. It was only recently that some of the instructors began to draw and design charts that were not confusing for a layman to understand.

They spotted the Western Sea; Jacqueline placed her thumb on it to mark the point, and Shalmar traced a route from Midbay that connected to it. With a slow movement of her index finger, Shalmar drew a line until it linked with the Numinous Sea, the sea that ran across the island of the mages.

But the Numinous Sea line didn't connect with any other line or land. For the first time, Shalmar and Jacqueline were confused as they peered at the chart of information.

"This is not right." Shalmar examined it again, just in case she missed it the first time. It was the same result.

"It is not just dangerous, but unwise to journey into a sea with no bearing whatsoever." She thought about the deal she had brokered with Sym, the reality of it dawned on her.

Had she come to this place for nothing.

As she gathered up the papers to store into the compartment, Jacqueline spotted something.

"Wait," touching Shalmar's arm softly as she directed her to put the map back to the table.

Shalmar unfolded it and watched Jacqueline with admiration. This was why she was glad that Jacqueline came along. She was her visual conscience and moral compass. The one who asked the important questions. The one who saw things that did not want to be seen.

Jacqueline grabbed the lamp and brought it closer to the map. "Here." She gestured to the point where the line ended. "What do you see?"

Shalmar had glanced over that point twice already. If there was something the young warrior was seeing, she intended to see it as well. Her sharp gaze fell on the map, and she studied the line properly. After several seconds, she sighed.

"I cannot find anything," she threw her hand up in frustration.

"Exactly," Jacqueline chuckled as she watched the little theatrics Shalmar displayed. "What happens when you turn the map upside down and trace that particular line?"

Shalmar raised her eyebrows. "You could've just told me to check the map upside down."

"I could have," Jacqueline cocked her head. "But I'm supposed to be the naughty one, remember?"

Shalmar couldn't help but laugh. She knew Jacqueline was trying to make her loosen up. It was becoming difficult since they left the meadow, but Jacqueline knew it was important. Her sister was in danger, and her fate hung in the balance of her actions or the lack of action—Shalmar couldn't save her if she wasn't focused.

She heaved a sigh and inverted the map. Jacqueline brought the lamp closer.

There, overlapping the Numinous sea dot, was another dot faintly visible. Shalmar grabbed the magnifying glass and peered through it.

A puff of air slipped out of her lips. "It is not a dot. It is a line."

"What does it say?"

"To Worlds Unknown," Shalmar raised her brow. "Nothing else. This can only mean one thing."

"Gilskian explorers haven't gone to explore those parts?"

"Exactly," Shalmar's eyes went over the route they must take. "There are unexplored lands beyond the Numinous sea, and if my vision was accurate, I will find my sister beyond these waters."

"And stop an impending doom apparently," Jacqueline smiled.

Without warning, Shalmar flung her body into the arms of the young warrior and kissed her mouth deeply. Elated, she held on to Shalmar and matched her hungry kiss. After an intense release for both women, they cleaned up the maps and chairs that they had scattered throughout during their passion.

Laughing sheepishly, they left the vaulted chamber, which was slightly less unkept than before they had fulfilled their desire for each other.

# CHAPTER THIRTEEN

It was the drone of the lapping waters that filtered through the walls that woke her. Yawning, she stretched and slipped out of bed. It was morning, and in the city of Turonia, the city of the Water Element, that meant training had begun in full force.

Turonia was a majestic city, a celestial glory. The streets were paved with the finest cobblestones and seashells which flowed from one street to the next. All the houses were the same, save for the royal castle situated right in the middle of the city.

It was an adventurer's delight—many glorious cliffs overlooking a crystal-clear lake. On the great walls of the city and some walls of various buildings, painters paid obeisance to All and every other god that had blessed them with creativity, by painting the walls with colourful arts.

The townsfolk typically lived in harmony and saw themselves as a unit and progressed exponentially. There was not a case for vices, for everyone knew the importance of contentment.

Legend had it that All, seemingly impressed with their progress as a nation thus far, had blessed them with a gift: the power to control and manipulate water. And so, in every family, there was a girl or boy who could invoke the power of the water element.

These people were specially trained under the tutelage of the chief, Harmish Greywater, ruler of Turonia. They were called the REFWE (The Royal Elite Forces of the Water Element). They were the unofficial bodyguards of the chief, even though he had no need for bodyguards.

For the most part, the training in Turonia was a rudimentary necessity for everyone. However, the people had the option of choosing to remain in the force and learn more sophisticated techniques or go their own way.

Until recently, the influx of members in REFWE was at a low. Turonia and the neighbouring water tribes of Torton, Jamokk, and Radnok had always maintained a lasting peace between them, so joining the force wasn't in high demand.

Recently a band of delinquents were rounded up at the gates and remanded in prison. Since then most of the townsfolk had enlisted to join the force to master their skills and work with water.

Princess Fernella moved to the window and peered down at the group of people who had gathered at the shores of one of the lakes. She spotted the chief at the head of the small gathering. He was saying something to the people, but he was too far away for her ears to pick it up.

After preparing herself for the day, she strode out of the room. Her heart was greatly troubled. Her mind, like wild horses, wandered to the screams of her people miles away in Jadehollow. It was being held under the rule of Greenflack, the devil of a cousin.

Ever since she came here with Lambord Redfear—the Passer King who had rescued her from the clutches of Greenflack—she wondered how they fared. She thought of her old stepmother, Oakina, and a tear trickled down from her eyes.

Oakina had looked after her as though she was her own. Fernella was too little to remember the events that led to her father taking Oakina as his mate, but from her deductions, it wasn't farfetched.

Her father, the deceased king, never muttered a word about her real mother. There were days it would seem as though he was going to reveal details about her birth. But just as she pressed for details, he would avoid the topic in totality and kept the high silence.

This he did till his eventual demise.

Oakina had told her that her father had come back to Jadehollow in the wake of the death of the reigning king, his father. He was looking weary and dishevelled with a small child in his arms. Fernella. She had catered to her and groomed her into a beautiful, strong princess.

In hindsight, Fernella felt sad that she couldn't stand and fight for her people. She wondered what they would think of her.

As she walked through the hall leading to the entrance of the castle where she resided, she heard a mirthless laughter reverberating through the walls.

She paused in her tracks and listened. Curiosity enveloped her, she changed her direction and took a flight of stairs into the under structure of the building that had recently become a makeshift prison.

As she glided down the stairs, she could hear their voices. As soon as they heard her footfall, they paused and lapsed into silence.

Seven men were seated in one of the cells separated by a huge metal blockade. They were ceased by the night watchers who found them inspecting the great walls of the city. They were brought in for questioning and refused to divulge any information as to where they had come from. They were immediately thrown behind bars.

"If it isn't the crowned princess of Jadehollow," one of them proclaimed. He was Em, the right-hand man of her nemesis. "Your people have starved us for over two days in a bid to force us to talk. Well, listen to this."

The princess just stared at the prisoners, relieved that they were out of reach from the metal blockade.

"Escaping to this place will be the single biggest mistake of your life. Our master Greenfleck grows more powerful every day, and he's coming for you to make a primary mate out of you."

"That will be over my dead body," Fernella barked in fury.

"You can only delay your fate," Em gave a wave of his arm. "You cannot deny it, princess. A strong power grows inside him, and whether you like it or not, he's coming here. He will have you for himself and lay waste to this beautiful city."

"What are you even talking about?" Fernella blurted out. "What powers? How does he have powers?"

"You were gone when it happened. Remember the Dolchie that has been in your family for years? The oracle of the all-seeing All? Our master slaughtered it and now has the power of the oracle flowing through him."

The colour drained from her face. A short shrill sound escaped her lips. She quickly quieted herself and gained her composure as to not show these men any weakness.

"You only have two options," Seeing his words had the desired effect he continued more dramatically. "Surrender. Leave for Jadehollow now and embrace your fate as the primary mate of our master. Delay it and watch him destroy you, together with this land, permanently."

Fernella couldn't wait to leave the place. She hurriedly advanced to the upper levels of the building. As she raced back, she heard his voice echoing through the walls.

"You cannot deny your fate."

A devilish laughter erupted, sending chills running down her spine. She didn't stop running until she got outside the building. She never broke her strides.

The cool breeze now swimming into her lungs did not slow her. She headed straight for the chief. A few of the Royal Elite Forces sensed what was about to happen and jostled through the crowd and barricaded the chief just in time to prevent bodily contact from the princess.

"Chief," she nodded her head in a hurry. "Sorry for interrupting you. I request to speak with you."

The chief, hearing the urgency laced in her voice, commanded the guards to make way. He took the hand of the princess, and they walked on the sands by the water. Some of the Elite Forces began following them. The chief turned to expel them.

They followed but kept a respectful distance—not close enough to pick up any conversation, just close enough to rush to his aid.

"What is it, princess?" his cool fatherly voice washed over his features.

"I fear that I have placed you and your people in grave danger."

The chief was greatly concerned by her words, but his stoicism remained. "What has made you draw that hasty conclusion?"

Fernella took a moment to focus herself. "Those tyrants found at the gates. I am the one they followed here. My cousin, Greenflack, is planning to attack this city if I don't agree to be his primary mate."

"Calm down now," Greywater was tapping her shoulder gently.

"The power of the Dolchie now flows inside him, and he has gotten powerful, more powerful than you know."

"And how did you come by that information?"

Fernella shifted as she spoke. "They told me everything. Greenflack will lay waste to this land, they said."

Harmish Greywater signalled the princess and began to slowly proceed on the sand. It was not the emotion she had expected from the chief. She expected him to be concerned, to bark commands to the guards, to secure the gates and shut everything down.

She quickened her pace and caught up with him. "You're not going to say anything?"

"Everything you have told me, I have found out on my own," His words seemed to surprise her. "The very moment he made the abomination of killing the Dolchie, I sensed it in my spirit. A distant signal that a great crime had been committed had come over me. I had mistaken it for the things one experiences in old age."

Fernella regarded the man before her. Though parts of his skin were wrinkled and the lines on his forehead were creased, the result of endless broodings, he still looked young and could handle himself well.

"I am much older than you think," he started moving again. "Now, when you stumbled here with my brother in-law, Lambord Redfear, my convictions became more apparent. Lambord explained much to me."

At the mention of his name, Fernella flushed and looked away. She remembered how he had rescued her against her judgement. She remembered how they were in such proximity of each other, his protective gaze poring over her as she slumbered.

She couldn't help but develop a type of fondness towards the Passer King. He was unlike any man she had ever met. His intentions and motives were pure and noble, she noticed. The way he looked at her intrigued her. In the coming days after he had brought her to Turonia, she saw it in his eyes that he struggled with restraint, to not say the wrong words to her. That fascinated her more.

It was the way their gaze had held when he told her he was going back to Jadehollow to free his men from captivity, stubbornly refusing assistance from the chief.

"And shortly after, those lowlifes were caught at the city gates," the chief's voice, breaking through her stream of thoughts. "Then I knew for sure, trouble was nigh. I had summoned a council of elders and told them of the recent development. We concluded," he stopped walking, "if anybody brings the fight to us, we will do whatever it takes, expend all our resources to retaliate and extinguish any flame. My people have lived on this land for many centuries, coexisting peacefully, and we plan to sustain that tradition for all eternity.

"Our guards," pointing to an elite guard who had mistaken the gesture for invitation and started marching towards them. Greywater dismissed him. "Our warriors are already enthusiastic about fighting, security at the gates has tripled, and I am getting my people sensitized on what to do in the event of a war.

"Now, I know what's going through your mind. That you have brought this upon us. What you need to realize is wars are bound to occur, sooner or later, whether we like it or not. The least we can do is prepare for it in the best way we can. Don't lose sleep over it. Walk with me."

Fernella walked with the old man, and the occasional sound of laughter flowed into the air. His reassurance was overwhelming as he kept a straight face with his hands crossed behind him. But her eyes pierced through his thick resolve.

And she knew that Harmish Greywater, the Chief of Turonia, was frightened.

# CHAPTER FOURTEEN

Greenflack was not a man known to be weak. Before he had the powers of the Dolchie flowing inside him, his band of thieves regarded him as a man who was concise and thoughtful.

Before he and his crew of misfits robbed any home, he always had a plan. He would also devise a backup plan if everything went sideways. It was this alertness, this ability he deployed on every raid, that made his cohorts respect him more.

As he sat reclining his back against a tree, he knew he was out of options. He could see the town of Jadehollow in the distance. His men were patrolling the grounds, swords at the ready, and a wistful smile spread across his lips.

The Fragahns wanted no part in his plan to bring destruction to Turonia and make Fernella his primary mate, sealing his rule over Jadehollow. The energy that was inside him was powerful, but it wasn't potent enough to bend the Fragahns to his will.

Launching an attack on the Turonians by himself would be risky. He wasn't sure of the tricks they had up their sleeves. Caution and restraint were his watchword now. He needed assistance, and it was not the kind that his remaining comrades at Jadehollow could offer.

As he sat and pondered his next course of action, he heard a rushing sound. It was almost midday, but the sky was beginning to darken, the clouds heavy with rain. Thunder boomed overhead and streaks of lightning flashed across the sky

The air bristled before him with so much intensity that the leaves of the trees blew off. He could sense the magic, and he knew it was not his own.

In a matter of seconds, a whirlwind emanated from the bristling air, its heights reaching higher. It remained in one spot, swirling and picking up dried leaves that were lying around. For a moment, he thought the Fragahns had come to finish him off. He stood up immediately, threw his arms in the air and concocted a dome of protection over himself.

A blue light flashed and began to glow. From inside the dome, Greenflack could make out the features of a man stepping out from the whirlwind. On second glance, it was more of a shadow than a human. Greenflack had not seen anything like this before, and his bravery was beginning to wane. He could hear his heart pounding in erratic heaves as the shadow proceeded towards the dome.

A moment passed between them. The silhouette peered at the man in the dome. It sensed the magic and the aura all around him. It began to beam. Finally, it had found a match—a match to bring its power to full potential.

Greenflack shivered in fright as the shadow stepped into the dome. He knew then that this creature wasn't a Fragahn. The whirlwind withered down and disappeared. The dark clouds cleared, and the sky became bright as day. But the dark form didn't move an inch. It was impossible to make out a face, because it wasn't there.

Everything happened in a matter of seconds. Greenflack's shivering lips parted and his mouth flew open on its own volition. Sensing what was about to happen, he tried to close his mouth, but it was as if it were glued open. He watched, mouth agape in fright, as the figure glided in the air. Greenflack tried to protest, but he couldn't move. He could not even form words inside his mind.

With a whiff of impatience about it, the dark form descended into Greenflack's mouth and swarmed inside his body. His mouth clamped back shut involuntarily, he felt the power stirring and bubbling inside him like soup in a cauldron.

Greenflack could feel the creature stretching his innards, filling every part of his body. He could feel the power swimming to his head filling his thoughts and his heart thrashing against his ribcage. Then everything went silent.

He heard the voice in his head.

*I am Declavius.*

It felt surreal hearing a voice inside him. It sounded ancient. While he sensed that it was the voice of a wizened old man, he felt a tinge of youthfulness in it. He gasped as he tried to gather his thoughts together. "My name is Greenfla—"

*Oh, I know who you are. Vibrant. Young. Wicked. Just like me. Some of your ideologies do not sit well with me, but I cannot fault your actions.*

Greenflack wondered how the voice in his head knew about him. Declavius, reading his thoughts, spoke again.

*Do not fret. I have gleaned through your memories. I have seen what you have done to clinch power. A lot of sacrifices. You are brave, maybe the bravest human I've seen in a while, which is a long time, considering that I am well over 700 years old.*

Greenflack measured his words properly before he spoke slowly.

"Are you a mage?"

*Yes, I am,* the voice was amused. *You will find out everything in due time. I can see that you have a minor issue before you. Your would-be primary mate is seeking solace in Turonia, and you're planning how best to raze the town to ashes and marry Fernella. I love your plans. I am willing to help you accomplish them. I will release my powers, and combined with yours, you will unleash unimaginable feats.*

"I am sensing that you have a proposition," Greenflack now eager for this new plan. All feelings of frightfulness wiped away from him.

*I have. I will help you, if you agree to help me.*

Without giving it much thought. "I will do anything if you keep your word."

*So be it.*

Greenflack felt the new energy that had entered him mingle with the powers of the Dolchie inside him. This new power was now becoming a part of him.

In an instant, he began to see memories. Not his own, but of the voice that spoke in his head. It was as though he was reliving his life.

He saw himself in a courtyard with older people practising the ritual of spreading their arms, emitting magic all around them. He was little, but the same magic that flowed through the others flowed through him as well. His body was moving on its own volition and he realized that his body had taken the form of the mage inside him. He was now of average height with long flowing robes. From all indications, he was the youngest of the group.

Greenflack couldn't process all that was happening, but he loved all his eyes saw.

They were casting spells on some terrified townsfolk. They had commanded a beast to rise from the ground to devour them. He was excited that a beast he had commanded was pulling a man apart.

The memory shifted to that of a great war. He was fighting with his comrades against an army of men riding on horses. The mages gained the upper hand, conjuring spells and jinxes to hurl at the humans.

The atmosphere changed when a lone rider rode to the middle of the battleground, carrying a small statuette. He raised it in the air and spoke in an ancient tongue, which Greenflack now understood. It was the spell of ostracism.

He saw magical clamps shoot out of the statuette, encircling his whole body. It was sizzling hot and he screamed in pain. He tried to get out of the contraption that had fastened around his body, the more he tried, the more the chains bit into his flesh. He looked around; his other comrades were trapped.

Then one by one, they started disappearing from the field. He was then transported to an island far from the lands they had once dominated. They gathered together to build a castle to protect themselves from the blistering northern wind. Once established, they started a ritual of revival in the great hall.

The memory shifted. He was traversing over lands on a mission to retrieve the damned Tarlaeth statuette that had rendered them captive on the island. Greenflack saw everything that had transpired—the battle inside the burial room of the Kings. The Tarlaeth. The King. He had trapped two women, Greenflack now knew them to be Amazons, and was about to bring extinction to it all. He noted one Amazon had started to defeat his power just as a rider crashed into the room. He repaired the statuette, commanding a spell that would shear his body in half. It was over for him in moments.

Greenflack now knew what the spirit of Declavius wanted. Revenge. He smiled. The plan was outlined in his mind. He would go to the coast land and cast a spell on the guards who would steal the Tarlaeth and destroy it, freeing other mages from the statuette's spell. With their combined powers, the mages would reconstruct his body, and he could possess it and destroy everyone who had stood in his way the first time.

He blinked and came back to the present. The power inside was oozing within him, begging to be commanded.

The consciousness of Declavius had moved on to entomb itself at the back of Greenflack's mind. He had offered up his powers for Greenflack to possess and control.

His eyes flitted to a patch of grass before him, and he channelled the energy inside him towards it. A dark red wave of energy shot out of his hands and the leaves of the grass began to extend inch by inch. A grin widened his lips as he watched the leaves transform from a stalk into a serpent with many heads. It was a fierce-looking hydra. Its many eyes were fixed on its master.

Greenflack burst into laughter. It was a long derisive sound that travelled throughout the woods.

He had not felt this way in a long time. For the first time since he and his men forcefully took control of Jadehollow, he could feel it in the air, wafting into his nostrils. He stared at the creature slithering towards him and took a long drag of air and sighed, heaving his chest.

Victory.

He could smell victory.

# CHAPTER FIFTEEN

It was almost noontime when the Amazon warriors stumbled into Midbay and spotted Noieh standing beside a boat at the dockyard. It looked new. It was well stocked with food, water, and other necessities they would need on their journey.

Noieh was quite elated that the warriors had picked her to embark on the journey with them. Considering they were Amazons who had special training negotiating dangerous waters, it was an honour to be thought of. She had felt less useful in the coming days after she had taken them to the shore where they had continued their journey to reclaim the Tarlaeth.

After settling their gear in the boat, they had begun sailing. Shalmar, with the assistance of Jacqueline, had produced a new map that Noieh fully understood. It was tricky for the most part, but she knew these waters, even more than the passengers she conveyed. She paddled gently towards their destination.

As they navigated, they began to discuss how the previous days had been. Shalmar was quite edgy about this area; she wasn't sure who else to trust when it came to divulging details about her past or her powers. From the dedication and focus that

Noieh had shown them on their last mission, Shalmar could feel in her gut that she was a loyal ally to them both and as their conversation progressed, she let Noieh in on the details. She took the information in, asking questions that made it certain she believed fully in magic and lifetime connections. This made Shalmar and Jacqueline aware that she knew and understood the relationship they shared.

For her own part, Noieh regaled them with the tales of a recent anomaly that had happened two moons ago in Midbay. They listened as she spoke about a farmer who was attacked by one of his own bulls at the entrance of his shed.

Why the story seemed sinister was because she said the bull was found beside the man, charred inside out. Noieh had concluded that magic had something to do with it. There was no other explanation.

Shalmar made a mental note to inform Sym after their mission, if she hadn't known about it already.

Jacqueline had been quiet throughout. She smiled as Shalmar was narrating what had happened at the hut. She considered what Shalmar had told her about her dream. For her dead father to appear to her in a vision to direct them on their current mission was not a matter to be handled lightly.

She was thankful that Shalmar now had powers. It was an edge. She didn't know whom they were up against or the kind of machinations they employed.

Shalmar noted the silence of her partner. Their gaze collided and Shalmar could see the love in

Jacqueline's eyes. With a reassuring smile, she touched her hand. A warmth passed through the friction and Jacqueline became more at ease.

The sun had gone down, and their stomachs groaned with hunger. Noieh had stocked the boat with plenty food. Jacqueline fixed them roasted meat and mead from the pouch, they passed small talk around.

Several miles in the distance, the Numinous Sea glinted in the darkness.

***

Her slippers pounded on the hard earth as she ran from the thing that chased her. It was impossible to see where she was running. She had no idea where she was, but she banked on her instincts to move her away from the creature breathing down her neck.

Her white robe flapped in the wind as she pushed herself forward. It was difficult to gather her thoughts when she felt like prey. Beads of sweat streamed down her body like a second skin.

In the bleakness, her foot met a twig, which sent her body crashing to the ground. Her face was pale with panic as she stumbled to her feet. A long scaly hand reached out and held onto her leg and dragged her body across the cold ground. She tried to scream for help, but it was as if her vocal cords were crushed. She tried fighting it off, but it seemed useless. It felt like a force of energy pulling at her rather than just a physical being.

She felt frozen as it hauled her to her feet. The thick arms turned her around. A face with blood lines erratically spreading across it as its eyes shone blood red.

*You are mine.*

Greenflack.

His hand lodged on her neck and clasped down on her throat, trapping the air inside her. With the firm grip on her neck, he hefted her in the air. She saw her vision blur as her feet dangled helplessly mid-air.

He squeezed hard again; she could see herself drowning in the murky waters of darkness. She tried to fight but her body was immobilized.

She was fading and heard a loud whinny followed by a strange chant. Then she heard a crashing sound and the grip on her neck slackened. She fell to the ground, gasping for air. Her ears picked up a howl of pain, the voice belonged to her attacker.

She wondered what had happened as she massaged her neck. Her eyes adjusting to her environment. The sound of retreating footsteps filled the silence of the woods. She knew it had to be Greenflack.

When she rose to her feet, her gaze levelled with a female warrior sitting atop a horse. She wasn't sure if she should scream or be still. She chose to be still. The warrior jumped down from the horse effortlessly and approached her.

"All be praised, you're safe," she heard the warrior, her grey green eyes examining her. "Sister."

***

Fernella woke up, she placed her hand on her throat, feeling the pressure in it. She jumped out of bed and slid out of her room still wearing her nightgown.

She slipped through the darkness of the castle hallway and to the surprise of the guards at the entrance of the castle., ran past them. They followed her, but at a slow pace.

She raced towards the shore, her feet rising and sinking into the thick sand. She stopped running when the water caressed her knees. Her breaths slowed after a while, the water inducing a calming effect on her. She thought about the nightmare she had just experienced. The guards were close by allowing her space.

She reflected to her encounter with the tyrants they had captured and what they had said about their master. She was beginning to sense that Greenflack had obtained more than the power of the Dolchie, and the thought terrified her.

She recalled the horse rider who had come to her rescue and she was filled with fondness. She remembered the familiarity of her voice, the odd connection between them she had experienced. As she stood knee-deep in the waters of Turonia, she could still sense her presence.

An unusual confidence filled her as the water swirled around her. She sighed, easing the air out of her lungs.

Then she remembered the last word the warrior had spoken.

*Sister?*

# CHAPTER SIXTEEN

Over the mountains of Turonia and across the continent, the lone castle in the middle of the island of mages stood out like a pillar in the darkness. It was lifeless and dark, except for the small light that pierced through the glassy windows from the upper room.

Inside the ruinous castle and in the great hall, nineteen mages sat hooded around a small fire. It was time for their monotonous night ritual of renewal, and their faces matched the nature of their heart—old and sombre.

Many days had passed since a member of their fold, Declavius, had been sent on an important mission to retrieve the statuette. The statuette who's name they dare not speak out loud as it could cause them harm.

They held hopeful ambitions as the young mage flew off. They anticipated the power that held them captive would finally be released. They banked on Declavius's youthfulness and enthusiasm to finish the job and restore them to the deities they had been. That day never came and the skies above their heads never brightened. The power of the statuette that had been weakened became stronger than previous days.

They feared the worst had happened when they could no longer feel the spiritual presence of the young mage.

"Declavius has failed us," they chanted gravely as they rolled their heads sullenly around the fire. "He was never the chosen one. He has doomed us for all eternity."

In the coming days, they acknowledged their fate—they were going to live their last days in this castle, stuck on the desolate island. Their revenge plot had begun to look like a failed conquest.

In these last few hours, they again began to feel the presence of Declavius. It was clear that it was not his complete self, but they were elated that he had awoken once again.

They gathered around the fire and mumbled in a strange language, a language that had the power to make exist all things that did not. As soon as they finished chanting, the fire bristled with more flames. It rose up above their heads and started to flow down through their foreheads into their bodies. Their bodies jerked as they mumbled until all of them had been rejuvenated by the perpetual flames.

A crackling sound erupted, the fire sputtered off, rendering the great hall in pitch darkness. A few unintelligible gibbers rambled on until a voice barked.

"Silence."

The voices petered down; the hall quiet once again. The voice that had commanded them belonged to the chairman, the oldest mage of them all.

He snapped his fingers and the small light appeared at the middle of the gathering. With a slow movement of his head, he scanned their faces. Bewilderment draped over them. It was unusual for the flame to be extinguished when the gathering was not over.

The chairman understood what was happening.

"Brothers and sisters," his voice was raspy with age, "for hundreds of years, no human has ever ventured into these parts through the Numinous Sea to go to the Land of the Elements. For good reason."

He clapped his hands twice and a bright light appeared in the centre of the circle they had formed; soon, the light paved way for a smoky mirror that showed an eagle view of the island and the sea that flowed around it.

The view was beautiful, though the plains were devoid of vegetation. As the strong northern wind blew, one mage spotted an anomaly in the waters. A small dot, after careful inspection, was confirmed to be a boat conveying three persons, negotiating through the cold.

"We haven't been entertained for ages," one piped up.

"It is true. If the cold doesn't kill them, the Chibanka will."

Chibanka was a beast cursed to live out its days in the sea. Creating mayhem for the few sailors who managed to find the enchanted waters. It had resided, undisturbed, at the bottom of the sea waiting to bring the next seafarers to their death. Many of the mages present had seen how the beast had slaughtered unsuspecting victims in times past. It was almost certain the creature would strike again.

"We sit and watch," the chairman wore a sinister smile.

# CHAPTER SEVENTEEN

The north wind squealed and blew harshly across the water as Jacqueline directed the boat. The wind was blowing behind them, gliding them forward making the task easier. Noieh had grown tired from paddling and was taking a break. Rubbing her palms together, the friction creating warmth that managed to flow to the rest of her body.

They had been on course for a day and a half. With the deftness Noieh employed, they were able to cross the Western Sea moving far north smoothly. They were close to entering the Numinous Sea, according to the map the warriors had examined at Command Tower.

The air was chilled, and the waves splashing frigid water into the vessel made it unkinder still. They had thick blankets made of wool and fur draped over their shivering bodies to bring some warmth. Their energy was being used to withstand the cooler temperatures and to keep directing the boat forward. Communication was limited, but Shalmar, stationed at the rear of the boat, was deep in thought. She wondered how her life would have turned out if she had never been separated from her sister, Fernella.

She had no use for restraint when it came to fend off enemy troops. She held nothing back; she always pushed herself. Would she entertain such ideology if she knew she had a sister to return home to?

As she reflected on her thoughts, she began to feel an odd sensation in her stomach and an alertness came into her mind. She began to sense something was wrong. She glanced around, after a moment, she was satisfied that there was no one in sight. She pushed the thought aside. Trying to distract herself, she stared at her partner, only to realize that her gaze had been fixed on her all along. Jacqueline smiled at her as her efforts continued to skim the boat over the water. After a small instruction from Noieh, Jacqueline had stayed on course.

Shalmar was so fixated in the depths of Jacqueline's gaze that she missed the small shift evident in the water. Noieh was beginning to sleep, the sound of her snores mingled with the swirling water.

Another surge of uneasiness crept up. An alarm went off in Shalmar's head. What was she missing?

"Something isn't feeling right," Shalmar broke the silence.

Jacqueline turned her attention to her. Shalmar could feel her body tingle and glanced around. She heard the loud rushing of the water. Her heart skipped when she saw it rising from underneath her.

A scaly jagged head poked out of the sea followed by its elongated body. Time slowed down as Shalmar gasped.

"In the name of Poseidon, wha—"

She had never seen such a creature before, nor had she heard tales about it. It was twice the length of their vessel. Its jagged head glinted a bluish green under the daylight. The blue scales on its head covered its entire body, down to the sharp tip of its pointed tail. Its back legs were shaped like a turtle's and its front arms looked like deformed hands with large claws. The beast's yellow eyes glowered, catching the glimmer of day as it threw its head high. It was larger than any creature she had ever seen.

Jacqueline heard movement behind her as Shalmar yelled her name.

The beast opened its wide mouth, exposing rows and rows of sharp, serrated teeth. A black substance hurled out and drenched Jacqueline. Shalmar armed with her sword, moved towards her. Jacqueline struggled to stand and wipe the substance from her face. The beast clamped on to her arm and disappeared with her into the water. Shalmar heard her short piercing scream before the water drowned it out.

"Noieh" the hunter was stumbling awake. "Grab a paddle."

Noieh vaulted into consciousness. The tail of the beast slammed into the water, causing a booming crash and a strong wave. It got Noieh focused.

She grabbed the paddle hurriedly.

"What do we do?"

Shalmar felt a sudden explosion of energy filling her. She felt the power charging inside her as she stared at the slight impression—the spot where the beast had disappeared with Jacqueline.

"I will get her back if I have to fight Poseidon himself."

She took a long drag of the air, felt the substance mingling with the power welling inside her, she dove into the water. The sea was dark, the water felt thick, and it was a challenge to stroke through it.

She had learned how to sustain her breath underwater for a lengthy period, she hoped with her new gift, she would last longer.

A movement from the corner of her eye piqued her attention. She turned her head just in time to spot the tail of the beast rocketing off in the distance. With a burst, her body pushed frontward pursuing the creature. The beast was stronger and faster, much more used to the water. She closed her eyes and summoned her powers to aid her.

A purple spark appeared on her fingertips and she felt a surge of vigour resonate through her body. She sped up and the tail of the beast was soon swirling within reach.

With both hands, she held on to its tail firmly. The beast, sensing the new weight tried to shake her off. Shalmar was prepared for it; she wasn't going to allow it to succeed.

As the beast maneuvered through the water, Shalmar held on to the tail with her left hand and reached with her right for her knife sheathed against her waist. With a ferocity she hadn't experienced before, she stabbed the beast. She could hear the growl of pain muffled through the water. The more it tried to throw Shalmar off, the tighter she held on to the knife she had buried in its tail.

She removed the knife from its tail and targeted a spot farther up its scaly skin. She could hear its growl and, fuelled with satisfaction, she removed the knife and speared the beast again, pulling herself farther up its reptilian body. Jacqueline was in sight, covered in a black cocoon. Shalmar crawled through the black slime, struggling to find the point of contact between Jacqueline and the creature. She pushed herself to the other side of the beast and saw one of the small scaly arms that had grabbed Jacqueline. Her eyes were open and unmoving, her mouth agape letting water in.

She fumbled for her knife and brought it down hard on the tentacle like arm of the creature. Raw pain shot through the beast, it released a loud groan and its hold on the captive. Shalmar held on to Jacqueline, her power charging stronger than ever through her, she shot for the surface of the water.

Noieh spotted them at the surface and stirred the bow towards them. She pulled the unconscious Jacqueline into the boat.

The rage-filled beast followed them quickly.

Shalmar felt the creature approaching below her. As her hand made for her sword that Noieh threw her, Shalmar drew in all her power and launched herself into the air. The beast rose out of the water, a greenish substance oozing out of the spots where Shalmar's knife had previously pierced its scaly flesh.

Shalmar aimed for the spot between its eyes and descended on it. The tip of the sword dug into the flesh, poking down through its throat. Noieh watched the spectacle in awe and readied her bow. She rapidly fired a couple of arrows, and they found their way into the midsection of the beast. It growled out in pain.

Shalmar withdrew her sword from its head, and an arrow flew past her and sunk into one of the beast's eyes. The beast rumbled, exposing its midsection for Shalmar's blade to slice through once more. As the blade cut through its chest, more of the green liquid escaped.

The creature collapsed on the water, deflecting the boat as it sunk to the depths. Noieh observed Shalmar dive into the water after it, surprised as she had ended its life.

Within seconds, Shalmar emerged and climbed into the vessel.

"I needed my knife," she spoke coldly.

Shalmar pulled Jacqueline into her arms and wiped her bangs from her face. She could see the marks the beast had made and felt her heart fill with fear.

Jacqueline remained stiff, her body cold and pale. Shalmar placed her hand on her chest. Jacqueline's heart was still beating, but faintly. She feared she would lose her. Shalmar focused and drew up one last rush of power from within her.

She closed her eyes and concentrated on moving the energy. She felt her heart centre open and directed this incredible force of energy to flow through her fingers. She felt a spark dancing on her fingertips and a bright gold light appeared. She then directed the sparks to flow through her and into Jacqueline's body. After a moment, the colour in Jacqueline's skin was returning and her body was becoming warm. Shalmar focused as she could feel the life force strengthening within her. Jacqueline's mouth opened; a flood of water escaped.

Jacqueline made a long whistling sound as she sucked the air into her lungs. She coughed and more water spouted out. Her eyes began to regain the brightness they normally had, and her heartbeat grew stronger once again.

Shalmar removed her hands slowly from her chest. Their eyes held each other motionless as Shalmar could feel the tears moving down her cheeks.

"By All, I thought I lost you," Shalmar's voice barely a whisper as she tenderly touched Jacqueline's cheek.

"And I, you," their lips met briefly.

"That was the Chibanka," Noieh proclaimed as Shalmar helped Jacqueline sit up and get comfortable. She wrapped a fur over Jacqueline's shoulders.

"A what?" Shalmar raised an eyebrow.

"Chibanka," Noieh was stirring the boat with less vigour now. "I've only heard tales about it. I never knew it resided in these waters."

"The beast is no longer."

"Thank you," Jacqueline's eyes studying Shalmar. "I'd have been resting in the belly of that vile creature if it wasn't for you."

"In the name of All, as long as I breathe and this power flows through me, I will be by your side," Shalmar said as their eyes caressed each other.

The three women, after sharing some food and drink, sat in their own thoughts as the boat voyaged through the water.

"We still have much to cover before reaching land," Noieh announced as she paddled the boat, her lean muscles flexing with every movement. It was night and Noieh was fatigued.

Shalmar glanced at Jacqueline who had just awoken from a much-needed sleep.

"To Worlds Unknown," they both said in unison.

Shalmar was delighted that they grew closer to their destination. The map had been right after all. She made a mental note to draw more concise detail about the terrain, and the large wildlife, and hand it off to Sym when this mission of saving her sister was complete.

For Jacqueline, Shalmar's promise resonated in her head. She knew she meant well, but it made her feel vulnerable. It was odd for her to feel this way after the core Amazon training she had experienced, but she found herself liking the idea. Who wouldn't feel protected with Shalmar fighting by their side?

Since Shalmar came into her powers, Jacqueline noticed, she had begun to exude a self-awareness that was unrivalled. She had always had an overwhelming level of confidence, but with her new gift it was something more. It was a sort of assurance that the mission was to be completed successfully.

Shalmar was still trying to learn and understand this new energy she possessed. She knew the more she used it, the stronger it would become and the better she could control it. She sat in thought. While still, she summoned up this unique magic that she had received from her father. Tiny white sparks flowed out of her body and covered every corner of the boat. Suddenly, the boat began to pick up pace, scissoring through the water. Noieh shot a quick glance at Shalmar, and then at her oar, which was beginning to look useless in her grasp.

"Show off," she grumbled, shoving the paddle on the bottom of the vessel. "You couldn't have done that sooner."

The three of them laughed whole-heartedly.

# CHAPTER EIGHTEEN

It had been days since Lambord Redfear had rescued Princess Fernella from the clutches of her cousin, Greenflack. He had promised her that he would come back after he rescued his band of Passers from Greenflack's men.

He didn't know exactly which promise was more difficult—the promise of saving the few men that managed to survive Greenflack's onslaught and were held captive with the townsfolk or journeying back to Turonia to be with Fernella.

There were many other things he wanted to tell Fernella before he had left. His mouth opened, but the words never formed. For the most part, he felt stupid leaving as he did. It was for the best. His men who had survived were being tortured and her people were held captive. It was not the time to talk about feelings he wasn't sure were even going to be permanent in the first place.

He had camped at the south-eastern part of Jadehollow, a couple of miles from the river, and surveyed the whole town from this vantage point, keeping out of sight of the tactically advantaged men.

For two days, he had lived on the fruits that grew in the forest and drank water from the stream nearby. He was biding his time, waiting for the perfect moment to launch a surprise attack on the guards and free his men and the people of Jadehollow.

From his observation, he knew that Greenflack and a small number of his men were not in the town. He knew that Greenflack's obsession with Fernella would drive him to Turonia to fetch her. The thought made him ball his fists in fury. He would never let it happen—not while he was still alive. Greenflack's absence in Jadehollow afforded his men to do what they wanted with no supervision. Jadehollow, now under control of Greenflack's savages, was now ruled by anarchy with a total shutdown of values and dignity.

When Greenflack's men felt bored, they would bring out a couple of prisoners from the makeshift rickety prison they had previously built. They would order the townsfolk to entertain them with dancing. The compliant prisoners were ridiculed and harassed; those who were non-compliant were severely punished. Earlier the previous day, he had watched as the guards humiliated Queen Oakina, Fernella's stepmother, the widow of the king.

They had ordered her to dance and when she blatantly refused, one of them shoved her hard, sending the frail woman to the ground. Redfear had been watching from the top of a tree. He had wanted to jump down and bring destruction to the attacker, but he knew it would only get him caught. Then, he wouldn't be able to help them at all.

He had never been a violent man. Violence was not in his blood; his father and his father before him were known to be tranquil beings, and they had taught him the same values.

Things were different now. Half of his men had already been eliminated. The people were being held captive, and the princess was going to be forced to become a primary mate.

*By the mighty All, I will not let it happen,* he reaffirmed.

As he pondered how best to approach the village before him, he heard a splashing sound from the distance. He turned to the direction it was coming from which was the sea. The water was lapping gently at the shore. He smiled. Just as his gaze shifted to Jadehollow, he spotted something in his peripherals. He couldn't see it clearly, but it was moving towards land. The early morning light was allowing his eyes to focus easier. It must be a boat, but it was speeding faster than a boat should be able to move. He gasped and rubbed his eyes as he could not believe what he was witnessing. It was a boat approaching shore, but he had never seen a vessel garner speed such as this. To make it even more unusual it was moving like this while the waves were flowing against it.

He thought it was a mirage, after blinking several times he knew it wasn't. There were tiny white sparks in the shape of a dome all around the vessel. It appeared to be magically speeding towards the shore without the assistance of anyone. When it docked, the white sparks shifted and flowed into someone with their arms outstretched.

All three passengers poured out on land. All women, he reckoned. He hadn't seen their kind of dress before. Two women wore similar clothing, the third something slightly different.

As he watched, they stood still for a moment glancing around the forest. As they shifted, the sun reflected light on objects on their waists. He looked as closely as he could from his perch in the tree and found the gleam to be blades and swords. The one dressed differently from the others carried a bow and quiver.

They were not just sojourners exploring a new land, he mused. They were warriors of some sort. As he stared at them, he realized that they may be from the Amazon Tribe he had heard of. Tales of their kind were told by many; their heroics, bravery and masterful skills were told by storytellers around the world. His attention was taken momentarily by a loud cry echoing from the town. He knew the guards had started whipping some unfortunate townsfolk.

He threw a quick glance towards the new visitors far away and an idea crossed him.

He mulled it over quickly and knew the risk was very high. But it was a risk worth taking. Slowly, he started climbing down the tree.

# CHAPTER NINETEEN

The sun was slowly receding on the horizon when the boat eased to a stop. A couple of shore birds flew away to safety. They all took a moment to take everything in.

Noieh scanned the shrubs, satisfied that the stillness of the forest before them was natural, she stepped out of the boat. The moment Shalmar stepped on land, a sudden jolt shot through her, flowing from her forehead to her toes.

"We are getting closer to Jadehollow," she spoke quietly. "I can feel it. From all indications, we are going to be facing a town surrounded by enemy forces." She turned to face the duo. "Tact must be employed at all times. I do not want to lose either of you, and I will try not to die here. Shall we?"

Shalmar's words particularly grabbed Jacqueline. She had seen the length Shalmar went to rescue her from the clutches of the beast. She also knew Shalmar would respect her and Noieh's abilities to handle themselves on their own.

They started venturing into the woodland. The canopy leaves shielded them from the sunlight, casting large shadows on the ground. A warm breeze blew across the forest, unsettling the vegetation. The warmth was welcoming as they could feel their limbs gaining heat.

Noieh was marvelled with the way the warriors moved; they were walking fast but their feet treaded lightly on the dried leaves, generating minimal noise. She even noticed that their footprints barely made a mark on the soft ground.

As a hunter skilled in tracking creatures, she knew that if the warriors didn't want to be found, they would not be. There were other things she had picked up from listening to them. Things that she knew if she applied to her hunting, she'd be matchless.

There was a small path that slithered through the forest. Shalmar led the way down the path, her eyes swinging left and right looking out for sudden movement. Jacqueline covered the rear, her fingers dancing around her scabbard. The hunter listened closely to the forest sounds, processing them as natural. Until her ears picked up a disturbance, making her freeze in her spot. It was sudden, but Jacqueline behind her was trained to react to sudden movements, or the sudden lack of movement.

Shalmar, on the other hand took another step forward and waited.

"Something is approaching us." Noieh was alert. "Something large, like a beast, walks this way."

"I sense it, too." Shalmar was in front, and her eyes never left the path. "Brace yourselves."

The forest was still and calm, save for the rustling of the leaves. Noieh thought the beast had stopped approaching and was poised to strike. Her hands flew to her back and grabbed the tail of an arrow, which she slung on her bow with lightning speed.

They were in a tactically disadvantaged position, Shalmar realized. There were in strange terrain, and whoever was watching them knew the topography. Her mind flew to the way the Zals had attacked them and carried them off to their king.

This was different. She had powers now.

She didn't have to close her eyes, lest become prey for whatever was planning to attack. She tapped inwardly to her power, and let it flow through her fingertips. The gust of wind flowed from her hands and rustled the trees in front of them, enhancing her hearing. As the breeze moved, she had a mental picture of the forest up ahead. Everything seemed fine until the waft reached a specific spot and meandered around it.

That was it.

"Whoever you are," Shalmar's voice broke the air. "Come out now, and I might consider a merciful death."

The forest remained still for a moment, and the cool breeze felt eerie. They all heard a pattering rising and a large man jumped into the path.

The upper half of this body was exposed, and they could see the intricate symbols that had been drawn on it. A sheathed sword was swinging low on his waist. There was no visible weapon nestled in his outstretched arms.

He looked mysterious, but calm, as he approached the trio.

"Take another step, and it will be your last."

There was a ring to Shalmar's voice. It had the required effect. He stood rooted to the spot; his hands still extended like a hawk. He had a soulful gaze that made Shalmar think he wasn't threatening.

"Who are you? And state your business," Noieh barked from behind Shalmar.

"I can tell you are strangers," he spoke calmly, his head bowed, but his face fixed to Shalmar. The two warriors moved up to stand by Shalmar's side.

"What gave it away?" Jacqueline's sarcasm evident.

"Let's start with your clothin—"

"You still haven't answered the question; I am pressed for time," Shalmar brushed in.

"If you insist," the man stood confidently. "My name is Lambord Redfear, King of the Passers."

The word struck a chord in the warrior's heart. Shalmar had heard it before in Amazon training when the history of the Amazons was taught. Her instructor, who had since passed, said the Amazons once collaborated with the Passers in ages that were as old as time. The Passers and the Amazons were allies and accomplished much good until their various quest drew them apart.

Since then, no one had heard of the Passers or had spotted them near the territorial boundaries of Gilsk. She didn't know what they looked like or the way they dressed. This man could be a fraud, and they could be walking right into a trap. It didn't feel as if it was though.

Noieh briefly inspected the man and noticed that there was a strangeness about him, and it was not necessarily bad or good. She found him intriguing.

"State your business," Shalmar's stare was firm.

Redfear stared at the three warriors and laughed to himself as he wondered how this would play out. Three women armed to the teeth with weapons of high-quality precision and the obvious skill to use them. They wouldn't waste time if he made a wrong move.

The woman who stood in front had an aura about her, a rare kind of fierceness he had only seen in one other person. Observing her, he was sure this was the one who had summoned the light in the boat. With that form of magic, he was hoping to make her his ally.

"A town a couple of miles from here is under siege." He was slowly raising his head. "Most of my band of brothers have tried to fend off the attack. The ones that were lucky to survive are being tortured and punished every day."

Shalmar knew where the discussion was leading, and she wasn't ready to comply with whatever pleas he would suggest. Nonetheless, she nodded for him to continue.

"The natives are imprisoned against their wishes. They can barely—"

"All right." With a wave, Shalmar cut him off. "State your business again."

Redfear sighed. "I need your help in restoring that city back to order." He took a step forward. As soon as he moved, an arrow whirred through the air and stuck beside his leg. It was a warning shot.

"What makes you think we will get roped into this war of yours?" Shalmar already knew the answer.

"Now that I think about it, I think All brought you here to this place for a reason," he spoke while gathering his thoughts. "Sooner or later, without my interference in your path, you will get to Jadehollow and you will encounter the horrors there for yourse—"

"What words did you speak?" Shalmar could feel her heart rising.

"The horrors of—"

"No, before that." Shalmar edged forward. "The name of the town up ahead."

"Jadehollow."

Shalmar tried to maintain her calm as she levelled her gaze with Redfear. She thought of her vision, the fears of what her father had said, had already manifested.

"The royal family, what about the royal family?"

"Queen Oakina is in dreadful condition. Her stepdaughter escaped with me just before the men took over the town."

Redfear had become aware of the uneasiness in the air. The warrior out front seemed to be concerned.

"The Princess," Shalmar's eyes borrowing deep into Redfear. "is it Fernella?"

"Yes," he answered noting the interest.

The mention of her sister's name sent shivers down her spine. "Where did you take her? How far is that place from here?"

"A day on horseback," Redfear said. "Please, help me reclaim the town, so I can get to Turonia with my men."

"Why?"

"Fernella's cousin, Greenflack, was the one who orchestrated this siege. I have had surveillance on the town for two days now. He and a significant number of his men have left town. He's staking claims to the throne, and he wants to forcefully make the princess his primary mate. Jadehollow is the town ruled by the element of air. Turonia ruled by water. This could also cause a great disruption amongst the balance of the elemental circle. Not to mention Fernella despises him, and rightfully so."

"Primary mate?" She hadn't heard the phrase before.

"Yes. It is the mergence of two souls at a higher level, beyond the physical realm. It is the embodiment of essence, energy, beyond this world. It only occurs with those who hold the gift of the elements, earth, air, fire, or water. It is a connection that exists through lifetimes." Shalmar and Jacqueline exchanged a penetrating stare. They both reflected upon their joining in the meadow and knew then that it had been of a different intensity. This confirmed it.

"Greenflack will stop at nothing to get to her. He also knows their joining will allow him the sanction of powers tied to the air element."

Shalmar returning her gaze to Redfear, attempted to mask the anger boiling inside her. Shalmar, motioning her comrades to follow, they began to speak in hushed tones. Noieh still had another arrow aimed at Redfear's forehead, daring him to take another step.

Shalmar was usually the one who acted with restraint, but she found herself cajoling the others to follow a stranger they had met only moments ago. Jacqueline didn't like any of it. For one, she wasn't sure if Redfear could be trusted, even though from his mere countenance he seemed noble. She could see a hint of sadness in his eyes. Perhaps it came from the reality of losing his men. Or perhaps he was telling a lie, and this was all a ruse to trap the three of them.

Shalmar, telling them of her knowledge of the Passers, convinced them that it was of their best interest. It was also the best way to find her sister, and she was going to use it to her advantage.

"We have agreed to join forces with you to take back Jadehollow,"

"By All. Thank you," Redfear proclaimed.

"It's going to be done by our terms." Shalmar smiled and went on to tell him the plan. While the women were fascinated by the plan Shalmar outlined, Lambord Redfear felt uneasy.

He didn't like it one bit, but if his sense of this warrior was correct, he would agree to go along with the plan. He knew it was the best option.

# CHAPTER TWENTY

The sky above Jadehollow was gloomy, just like the hearts of the townsfolk that had gathered that evening under the command of the men that had taken control of the town.

For the last few days, Jadehollow had experienced torture, sadness, and anguish. The loss of their king coupled with the massacre of their people had rendered them defenceless and weak. There was no one who had stood up to their attackers who still stood alive today. Their numbers were fast reducing, even their livestock were dying off in huge numbers and their crops withered and perished. Greenflack had placed a spell upon the town to be sure that no one of the air element could use their gifts.

The days moved slowly. By now, the thrill of torturing the natives had long gone, but it was their only source of entertainment as they waited for further orders. They lined the townsfolk up in twos and ordered them to dance outside the small town's square. The weary-faced natives carried out the orders, albeit languid with their feet.

Greenflack's men were determined to make them more compliant to their wishes. One of them rose up from his chair with a long whip clutched in his hand. He was about to thrash out at the frail looking people when he heard a thunderous noise. It was followed by whoops of jubilation.

Five guards appeared, manhandling a man in their midst. When the guards who were stationed at the square spotted the new visitor, they joined in the shouts of joy.

"We found him lurking in the farms this evening," one of the men said and shoved him forward. "He surrendered as soon as we spotted him. Greenflack will be happy about this."

Lambord Redfear was disarmed and out of options. He silently prayed that the visitors he had met would follow through with the rest of the plan. It was important they did, and given the current circumstances he was in, it was important they did so in a timely fashion. He still had no idea if his new friends were really of the Amazon Tribe. If they were, he would feel much more at ease as he knew the history of their people and his. In his gut, he sensed that the warrior who laid out this plan could be trusted with her word. Something about her seemed familiar.

One of the men walked up to him and smacked him hard on his face. It carried a heavy weight to it, and it sent Redfear crashing to the ground. The assaults came right after. As he tried to get back on his feet, another man kicked his midsection. Several more kicks later, he curled himself into a ball to protect his head and he groaned in pain.

"Bring his men forward," The leader commanded. "Let them watch us deal with their king."

A few men scattered and brought out the surviving Passers forward. At the sight of them, Redfear's tears flowed freely from his eyes. His men had been beaten to the point he had difficulty in identifying them. There were only seven left.

On second look, he could spot Roughier, the man who had taken care of him after his father's death. His face was swollen with several bruises, his movements accompanied by excruciating pain.

Redfear groaned in rage.

"This man here, your king, ran away with the princess like a coward, too scared to remain and fight with his men and protect their interest," Greenflack's man boasted. "He is no king. He is a disgrace that should be cleansed this moment. He shall die by his own sword." He glanced at his men waiting for them to present Redfear's sword to him.

They glanced around at each other like bumbling fools as none of them had come across his sword. Their nervousness growing as the leader glared at them, trying to hide his embarrassment of not being able to follow through with his words.

One guard piped up. "Uh, he was not armed when we seized him."

"Then he shall die by my sword," With a grunt he unsheathed his glinting blade. Roughier chose this time to speak. His voice was laced with sorrow, dragging slowly out of his lips.

"Dead or alive, he will always remain our king, like his father before him. And if you bring harm to him, bring that same harm to us all. For we serve this king alive or dead."

The guard exchanged incredulous looks between Redfear and the old injured man. His face broke into a smile.

"So be it." He nodded to the other man who brought out weapons and stood behind the enslaved passers. "On my command."

He raised his sword in the air and was about to bring it down on Redfear's neck when they heard a short whistling sound. Suddenly, an arrow was sticking out of his forehead.

Redfear looked at it and smiled. It was the same branded arrow that had stuck beside his legs deep in the forest.

Soon after, another arrow found its way into the man's chest and he crumpled on the ground, lifeless. The others were perplexed, too shocked to move. They looked around in fright and couldn't spot the archer.

The distraction in Shalmar's plan had worked the way she said it would. They were all in one spot, which made picking them off with Noieh's arrows easier. As Noieh shot another arrow from her bow, Shalmar and Jacqueline spread out in opposite directions.

Greenflack's men were still too stunned to figure out how to fight back. They all rushed to the centre of the square. As the arrows kept finding their way into the centre of the men, a few of them were smart enough to move in the direction the arrows were launching from. Redfear saw his chance. He quickly rolled away until his body was within the perimeter of the square.

Shalmar was waiting for him with his sword ready.

"Why did you wait so long before you got into action?" he grumbled.

"The others didn't trust you as much as I do. I just had to ensure that they were fully convinced." Shalmar was smiling. "Besides, you are fine. Shall we?" She handed him his sword, gesturing forward playfully. Redfear, shook his head smiling, intrigued by the confidence she exuded.

As if on cue, they stumbled into the square. At sight of them, Greenflack's men raised their swords and aimed for them. The thirteen men raced towards Shalmar and Redfear straight on.

Jacqueline navigated slowly around the other side of the perimeter to the back of the square. She paused, listening for any strange movement or sound. When she was sure that it was clear, she began to move again, making minimal noise as her boot brushed against the grass.

The makeshift prison came into view as she cut through the thickets. Glancing around, she crept to the gate. Some of Jadehollows people were still imprisoned inside.

With a swift motion of her blade, the rickety chains snapped apart. The clanking noise being drowned out from the fighting taking place. She gestured for them to move to the town buildings away from the prison. The distraction Shalmar and Redfear had created had paid off. None of Greenflack's men were paying attention to what was happening behind them.

Truthfully, Jacqueline didn't like the part she was playing in it all. Shalmar had reminded her that every part was equally important. She knew Noieh had taken a strategic position at the top of a tree and knew by now she had descended from her spot to assist further.

With the people of the town safe, Jacqueline approached the square, lithe as a cheetah. One by one, she aided the Passers to safer ground.

"Surrender now." Shalmar barked. "Or die in your madness."

One of the men stepped out. "If you haven't noticed, you bitch, you are greatly outnumbered and—"

"What did you call me?" Shalmar slowly moved towards him like a tigress stalking its prey.

"Bitch," the man grunted louder this time. It was accompanied by several chuckles. "And I will say it again, you bi—"

As Shalmar brought her sword forward, an arrow flew into his mouth, trapping the remaining part of his speech. It stuck right through the other side of his neck. The light went out of his eyes as he hit the ground hard, creating a cloud of dust. In the dizziness of it all, the men charged towards Shalmar and Redfear.

Redfear held on to his sword, more firmly this time, and stilled himself. Shalmar called on the powers that welled inside her. As it began to flow throughout her body, she started racing towards the approaching mass of enemies. When they were in close range, she launched herself in the air and unleashed her sword. The windstorm of dust and debris she created was a good screen for her and Redfear as they positioned themselves amongst the men.

Using a shield, she had removed from a dead guard, Shalmar descended in a blur. She bumped into the first man and smacked him out of the way with her shield. The force propelled him into the air and sent him crashing into the shrubs. Shalmar enjoyed the powers she possessed but still felt exhilarated to fight the way she was used to. She loved the burning sensation in her muscles and the swiftness in her sword.

Redfear followed quickly behind, they started fighting their way through Greenflack's men. Quick movement of their swords bit into the flesh of the men, and soon there were many mangled bodies scattered across the square. The wind was still high as they expertly took down each opponent. With a simple gesture, Shalmar tamed the wind once more.

Redfear sustained some minor cuts, but he paid no attention to them. Adrenaline pumped into him as he fought. Screams tore the air as crimson spilled out of the men he sparred with.

Soon after, their numbers reduced by more than half. Backing out now seemed like the only option for them. Together, the reprobates began to move backwards in a bid to escape. Their horses were tied to a shed just beyond the square. As they moved, Jacqueline appeared, blocking their path with her sword glinting in her hand. She had managed to rescue all the injured townsfolk from the prison and had led them away to the outskirts where Noieh was tending to them.

"I will not say it again. Put down your weapons and surrender," Shalmar shifted her sword. "Or meet your fate with Thanatos."

Jacqueline rolled her sword, daring them to make a break for it. Shalmar and Redfear stood still, waiting for them to decide their fate. One fool decided to take a run at Jacqueline, who quickly clashed her sword with his. After a few seconds of playful sparring for Jacqueline, she jumped up onto an old barrel and flipped herself up and over him. She pulled the blade of her sword expertly across the front of his throat, and he collapsed to the ground motionless. Shalmar met her gaze momentarily and smiled as Jacqueline shrugged comically.

The men briefly shot each other a knowing glance and concluded. One by one, they began to drop their weapons.

"You have violated this land and will face the full brunt of the laws of Jadehollow," Lambord Redfear stepped forward. "Any sudden moves, and I will not hesitate to show you what a slow death feels like."

As he began to escort them into the prison they had constructed, whoops of jubilation pierced the air. It was the townsfolk. Salvation had finally come. They started racing back to the town square, and men, women, and children were singing praises and dancing.

Shalmar beamed with joy as the people ran around and formed a circle around all four of them, their voices laced with happiness. Jadehollow was her ancestral home and these people were her people. One of the children raced to her side and raised her outstretched arms.

She smiled as she reached down and hefted the small girl into her arms. Then, all the children rushed into the spot and embraced the warriors and the Passer King.

Redfear cut through the sea of people and walked to where Shalmar was. "The queen would like to see you."

He led her away from the circle, past the writhing bodies on the ground to where a lone woman stood, clutching a walking stick.

"You must be Shalmar," the woman was smiling.

Shalmar gasped. She was sure she had never introduced herself to Redfear. How did the frail old queen know who she was?

"You are just as Ruther described," the elder woman walking forward and grabbing Shalmar's hand. "You have your father's eyes."

"You know my father?" Shalmar blurted, then realized the oddity in that statement.

However, the old woman never broke her smile. "My name is Oakina. I am joined to your father as his primary mate," she nodded. "In the sense of the word only as your mother, Sarith, is bound with him eternally." There was no regret in her wise eyes as she spoke.

The jubilation was getting louder and louder. Oakina, using her walking stick, shuffled away from the festivities. Shalmar stayed present beside her.

"Your father told me everything about you and your mother, Sarith. It was the sincerity and honesty in his heart that made me love him and agree to be with him. However, he made me swear not to tell your sister. I couldn't bear children of my own. Not that it mattered. I had your sister to take care of. I saw in her a daughter, and I watched her grow into a beautiful princess and heir to the throne. I know why you are here. Your sister is in grave danger."

Shalmar did her best to stay calm and focus on what was being said. She nodded grimly to Oakina. "I saw it in a vision."

"Yes, your father came to you. You must know what you are up against. Your far cousin Greenflack has done a despicable act; he took the life of a Dolchie." She saw the questioning look on Shalmar's face, she quickly added "An oracle. I have been having visions of Greenflack growing stronger. Only yesterday, I was flung into another vision. What I saw still frightens me now."

Shalmar focused all her attention on what the elder woman was saying. With the events that have happened, nothing came as a surprise to her any longer.

"Something evil now brews within Greenflack. Something ancient. He needs to be stopped. Your sister needs to be saved before it's too late."

"We leave for Turonia tonight," Shalmar nodded.

"You and your sister must work together to defeat him. I can sense your father's power flowing inside you. You are more powerful than you know. Hold nothing back. Now, I must join my people, your people, to celebrate. May All be with you in your conquest, and may you come back with your sister, my daughter." And with that, she walked back into the circle.

Shalmar signalled to Jacqueline, Noieh, and Redfear to join her.

"We ride tonight to Turonia. No breaks. No sleep."

"Without breaks, we will get there by noontide tomorrow," Redfear said. "My men are too weak to fight. They will have to remain here."

Shalmar considered the sudden development and shrugged. "Four of us may be all we need." She faced Noieh, touching her arm. "Fetch some horses."

Noieh nodded and left.

"Who are you people?" Redfear found himself asking. "From whence do you come?"

"I am Shalmar, and this is Jacqueline," she gestured to the woman who stood beside her. "We are

Amazon warriors." She paused to catch her breath and saw the recognition appear on Redfear's face. Then she continued, "Fernella is my sister."

Disbelief draped Redfear's face as her statement sank. "Amazons. I could see from your skills and bravery that you would be such. Our people had joined forces long ago. Now again, you appear by the grace of All." He stared at them for a moment and continued. "Fernella is your blood. That is why you seemed familiar to me."

"It's a long story. All of which I will explain to you along the way," Shalmar looked at the man before them. "I sense your struggle. Why is it that you fear the love you hold for my sister?"

Just then, Noieh came back, dragging the reins of four fit horses who tagged behind. After a quick introduction of Noieh and Redfear, they made sure they had all they needed. Shalmar familiarized herself with her new horse before departing.

They all mounted up and slowly began to navigate through the town. The townsfolk cheered on as they rode past them. Then the horses began to move at a galloping pace, the town slowly fading behind them.

"Cha," Shalmar commanded and the horse increased its pace.

# CHAPTER TWENTY-ONE

It was morning in Turonia when it happened. The daily activities had begun as usual, and the Royal Elite Forces had commenced their trainings under the supervision of Chief Harmish Greywater, by the riverside. The air was alive with shrills of children playing and running mindlessly beside the shoreline.

The night watchers had been relieved of their duties at the main gates and had been replaced by the regular guards. The guards who had replaced the night watchers were seated at the tower, chatting and throwing jabs around when one of them sighted a lone figure in the distance walking proudly. He motioned to the others, and they alerted the guards below doing the patrols.

Since the guards were tripled on the grounds, their new directive was stern. No visitor was to be granted passage into Turonia, except by the approval of the chief himself, and it was so for the last several days. Visits to Turonia were limited, and no one had any reason to leave the city.

Until now.

The guards exchanged looks briefly as the figure approached. The man wore a robe that covered most of his face, and his gaits were precise and filled of pride. When they were sure he could hear them, one of them barked an order.

"Remain still. Who are you and what brings you to Turonia?"

Greenflack burst out in derisive laughter. It was loud and piercing, and it travelled with the wind to the Elite Forces training beside the river. They stopped training immediately, fixing their gazes at the gates. The chief, sensing the worse, started walking towards the palace, the guards attending him followed.

The guards on the tower drew and aimed pointed arrows on him.

"Oh, I would not do that if I were you," Greenflack waved a hand.

"We will not hesitate to fire you down if you do not—"

"If I do not what? Leave? That will never happen." Greenflack matched their stares with his. "To answer your question, I came looking for a fair lady. Do you know her? She's a princess."

On hearing that, the men fired their arrows. Six arrows were spiralling towards Greenflack's head. He raised his left hand and all the arrows froze mid-air. The guards watched in amazement as their arrows swirled in the air, moving no further.

"Amazing, right?" an amused Greenflack smiled. "It took some time for me to master that. And if I remember correctly, I warned you not to do that. You have to pay for your disobedience."

With a flick of his fingers, the arrows turned and pointed towards the tower guards. Terrified, one of them hurried down the tower and started running away from his post.

With another wave of his fingers, the arrows flew back and shot through the foreheads of the stunned guards. Their journey to the afterlife was instant. The lone arrow that was left, magically scaled over the wall and began to trail its target. It soon caught up to its mark and pierced his head, sending his stupefied body to the ground.

The air was filled with horrified screams as the children at the shoreline started running haphazardly through the streets in search for their parents.

"Sound the alarm," one of the commanders of the Elite Forces barked. "We are under attack. Protect the crown at all cost."

It was the alarm that sent Fernella into consciousness. She knew why it was sounded—she had feared this outcome for days. The nightmare she had recently was still etched in her memory like an injury that wouldn't go away. She rolled out of the bed and quickly changed into her fitted gown.

She heard a loud knock on the door and the chief stumbled.

"Greenflack is here," he directed her out the door. "Come with me."

He led her through the large hallway, and into a smaller passageway she hadn't explored before. It was the chief's private quarters. He led her to the end of the aisle to a large rusty door.

Greywater rapped on the door twice. They heard a shifting noise inside. The door creaked and opened, revealing the wife of the chief and their two children. He pushed Fernella inside.

"Under no circumstances should anyone leave this place." It was a stern warning. "I am going to organize my men."

Against their protests, he swung the door shut.

Meanwhile, Greenflack stared at the closed high gates and his lips broke a smile. Over the past two days, he had learnt how to levitate, among the other evil things he had picked up using the powers of the Declavius the mage inside him. He was no coward. He would not soar over the fence. No, he would enter the city through its main entrance. If he wasn't going to be granted access in, he would force his way in.

He balled his fists and shot a burst of energy forwards towards the metal gate. The gate stayed put, but the hinges on either side had loosened. The guards patrolling the grounds were stationed behind the gate with their spears and poised to strike.

Another bolt of energy shot out of Greenflack's hands and the hinges came off. The metal gates blew apart and sent the guards standing directly behind it into the air. Some of them survived the fall; others crushed. The metal gates trapped them beneath its steely bulk.

Greenflack could hear the horrified screams as he stepped into the city. He could see the guards forming together in a protective stance.

A man came out of the line of defence. Greenflack deduced this was the chief.

"You are not welcome here," Greywater stood firmly "You have brought violence to our city."

"I will unleash more if you do not cooperate with me. You are keeping someone who doesn't belong here, and I have come here take her back."

"I cannot allow that" Greywater's rage was palpable all over his countenance.

"Then die in your folly." Greenflack threw his hands in the air and a massive ball of fire appeared. Smiling, he shot the ball of fire at the chief.

The Royal Elite Forces commanded water to flow out of their hands and they directed it to the approaching fireball. It sizzled and quenched before it reached the chief.

"Attack." the chief commanded.

Immediately, every member of the Force created bulbs of water out of their hands. They manipulated it, until they formed iced pointy tips and fired them towards the lone Greenflack. But a dome-like force appeared and covered his body, and the water splashed on the dome and sidled downwards. Greenflack was well protected inside.

"Again."

The men formed another set of iced spears and hurled it towards Greenflack who now sat cross-legged on the ground. Again, they watched perplexed as the spears bounced off the dome and plopped on the ground.

"I admire your resilience," Greenflack's voice boomed through the force field. "It humours me." He shut his eyes and called up the powers bouncing inside him. The ground vibrated under their feet.

"Shift back." The guards inched backwards waiting to see what was being brought forth. Greywater knew this to be a magic he had not witnessed before. It was of an ancient, and he knew they were not ready for this magnitude of power.

A large gap in the ground opened between them and the intruder. There was horror etched on their faces as they watched tentacles begin to crawl out of the hole. They were large and moved with terrifying speed. Some of the men were questioning the limits of their loyalty and bravery; when the chief had said the city would be under attack, this was not what they had envisioned.

Their horror intensified when one of the tentacles rushed forward to wrap around the neck of one of the men. He struggled against the tight grip, but it was useless. They watched as the tentacle hefted him in the air and dragged him into the cavity.

They heard a hollow beastly sound, followed by the blood-curdling screams of the guard. Before they could react, another tentacle had wrapped itself around the legs of another Turonian.

"Noooooo".

The soldier struggled, digging his fingers into the dirt, but the hold on his limbs was firm. Another tentacle entangled around his other leg. He knew then that it was over.

"Save yourself. Save the crown," he screamed as he was pulled into the pit.

The tentacles began grasping at anything in the creature's path, pulling it inside the gaping hole. The archers were now in place, arrows flying endlessly but the skin of the beast was thick. Some arrows causing damage but not enough to slow it down.

"Swords," Harmish Greywater cried, snapping the men out of their bewilderment.

The brave warriors drew their swords. Some of the highly ranked officers had formed a circle around the chief. As the tentacles slithered forward, they all swung their swords, managing to slice off a portion of the creature. The dismembered limb left writhing on the ground.

An agonizing growl went up in the air as the wounded appendage retracted into the crater. They also noticed that Greenflack was twitching with discomfort as they hacked more tentacles. Charged up, the Royal Elite Forces went about dodging the tentacles and cutting them down in the process

Greenflack, holding his side and stumbling, was clearly experiencing pain as he watched the massacre before him. They had been terrified before, now they were filled with righteous indignation to tip the scales as they realized that hurting the beast injured Greenflack. The beast withdrew all its appendages, disappearing into the earth as the ground closed.

"Fools," he cussed, the pain evident in his voice "Today, sorrow shall dwell amongst you."

He clapped his hands five times, each clap reverberating through the town. The Elite Force grouped together and was alert. They shot water darts from their hands and glanced regrettably as they bounced off the impregnable force still surrounding Greenflack.

Their faces were filled with shock when a bright red light danced before them. As it dissipated, there stood five hairless creatures in the form of lions, their red eyes glaring at the guards and their chief.

The beasts roared in unison; their large teeth bared as they slowly moved towards the forces.

"Fernella, listen to me," Greenflack's voice was amplified through the dome, so loud that everyone in the town could hear him. "Many people have died on your account today. If you want to add more to the rising number, be my guest."

He snapped his fingers, the beasts growled and started advancing towards the forces.

The Forces stood their ground at first, swinging their blades at the beasts. As the beasts advanced ferociously, many men suffered debilitating injuries and a greater number fell lifeless.

Some of the few commanders moved the chief away from the entrance of the city. The air was filled with growls and screams.

Inside the palace walls, the howls of pain filled Fernella's ears. A sorrow she hadn't known before draped all over her demeanour. She knew that all of what was happening was because of her. She wondered what would have become of Turonia if she had remained in Jadehollow. She shook her head. She was the cause of every misfortune Turonia was experiencing. Greenflack would not stop killing the good people until she surrendered herself.

She walked towards the door.

"What are you doing?" Molum, the wife of the chief asked. Her terrified children grabbed the helm of her robe.

"Saving Turonia," Fernella reached the door "This city has been too good to me, and I cannot repay it like this."

"No."

"Please, stay here, and lock this behind me," she swung the metal door shut. She bounded down the hall, hearing the screams grow louder. She navigated through the main hall and ran outside the palace.

When she saw the bloodbath unfolding in front of her, her body went stiff with fright. A hairless lion was tearing down a soldier too weak to do anything about it.

"Greenflack," she screamed above the noise. "You want me? You can have me. Leave these people be."

As soon as he spotted her, Greenflack snapped his fingers and the beasts vanished. Fernella ran through the lifeless and injured bodies, her heart pounding hard in her chest. A hand grabbed her bringing her to a halt.

"What are you doing?" the chief was stunned at her bravery. "It would be unwise for you to go to him."

"No, chief," Fernella touched his hand momentarily. "I cannot let you and your people continue to die for me." She slipped her arm out of his grip and stepped forward.

The men were too weak to use the opportunity to launch an attack. A significant number of them had died in the mouths of the beasts. The ones who had managed to survive were severely injured and unable to move.

"You have come for me," Fernella barked as she got closer to the dome. "Leave Turonia out of this."

"Fine." Greenflack smiled. Slowly, he rose to his feet. When their gaze met, a cold shiver ran down her spine. He was no longer human, she realized, staring at the red pupils that bulged in his dark eyes.

"The people of Turonia will bear witness that I, Greenflack, son of Unnoth, do take you as my primary mate to rule over all of Jadehollow and beyond."

"Over my dead body will I accept to be joined with you in such a meaningful way," Fernella proclaimed as she stood in front of him. Her eyes were as cold as steel even though she was scared.

"You would disrespect me in front of these feeble townsfolk?" He was glancing around with his arms in the air. He turned and grabbed her neck. Fernella gasped and tried to free herself, but her strength could not be compared to Greenflack's.

Realizing the dire situation, Greywater conjured up a spell and hurled it across at him. Again, like the others, it bounced off the dome.

Greenflack lifted her off the ground. "Since, you have decided not to bond with me, I have no use for you anymore. After I take your life, I will destroy this city."

As his palms tightened around her neck, a pounding sounded in the distance. It grew louder and, soon after, four riders appeared on the ruinous entrance of the city.

"Not on this day," said a powerful voice.

Before Greenflack realized what was happening, the gelding Shalmar was riding knocked him on the ground, freeing his grip on Fernella. The dome he had created disappeared.

Fernella wondered what was happening.

"Sister."

It was the same voice on her vision. She looked up to see a woman confidently staring down on her with piercing green eyes. Her face seemed familiar, even though she couldn't place it. Shalmar dismounted, releasing the horse to safety.

It was when she grabbed her arm that everything changed. It began to animate all the memories that had been long mummified. Fernella threw her head back as all the memories she had had with her sister came rushing back.

When Fernella opened her eyes and looked at her face again, her mouth slipped open. "Shalmar?"

"Yes," Shalmar smiled briefly. "Yes, Fernella. It is me."

The moment was short-lived. They heard the groans of Greenflack behind them and they knew that he had stumbled in consciousness.

Chief Harmish Greywater signalled his closest commanders, ordering them to wait for direction. Somewhere in his heart, he knew the scales had been tipped.

"I remember you," Greenflack growled angrily as his eyes rested on the Amazons. "Your deaths shall be swift."

He snapped his fingers, summoning three of the large grotesque creatures to charge towards them. The group dispersed. Jacqueline, directing her horse away from the others so a beast would follow and Redfear, seeing the princess close to her sister, darted the opposite way from them.

Noieh released an arrow from her bow as Shalmar charged it with energy; it hit its target in the space between the beast's eyes. Greenflack groaned as the beast dissolved.

One of the beasts was charging towards Jacqueline. She swiftly raised her sword, sprung up on her horse, spiraled in the air, and landed on the beast. Her sword plunging deep into its skull. It vanished and Greenflack began to scream in agony.

Redfear charged towards the remaining beast. It growled, raising its body in the air, its claws outstretched. He slid under it at the last moment and sliced its underbelly. It let out a loud roar and dispersed.

Clenching his fists, Greenflack yelled in an unknown tongue and a wave of energy shot from his forehead. The force blasted all five of them from where they stood, sending them crashing on the ground.

The Royal Elite Forces rushed to their aid and tried to help them to their feet. Greenflack blasted another wave of energy from his forehead, Shalmar was prepared this time. She conjured a web of protection over all of them.

Greenflack was surprised as his powers ricocheted and blasted him backwards. Begrudgingly, he rose to his feet. He started calling on the powers that were still inside him, summoning everything he had left.

Shalmar was aware of what was happening and allowed herself to focus. Greenflack, seemed to possess a magic she had seen before. He was chanting a powerful hex and she knew she had heard it in the past. She knew her powers alone were not enough to take him down. If she didn't act now, they all may very well die here.

She turned to look at her sister. The words of Oakina flooding her mind

*Something evil now brews within Greenflack. Something ancient. He needs to be stopped...You and your sister must work together to defeat him. I can sense your father's power flowing inside you. You are more powerful than you know. Hold nothing back.*

"Declavius," Shalmar grimaced his name out loud. Greenflack's eyes flew open. They were dark, lifeless and cold. He leered at Shalmar. "Yes, great Amazon. I have returned to claim what is rightfully mine."

Shalmar's mind was racing with possibilities.

"This will hurt a little," her voice was charming as she held Fernella's hands. Fernella suspecting what was happening, closed her eyes with her sister.

Shalmar started to recite a chant in an ancient language. It was the same language she heard her father speak when he had knelt beside her young sleeping form in the old hut.

As she chanted, she could feel the energy inside her swirling and moving to her fingertips. Slowly, it began to channel into her sister. Fernella jerked backwards as her body accommodated the torrent of energy that seeped into her.

After a few seconds, Shalmar severed the connection.

"That will last for a few moments, but it will be all we need to take him down."

Together, they faced Declavius. Fernella followed Shalmar's lead. Greenflack's forehead was glowing bright red. In the ensuing second, a bolt of dark magic shot out of his head and aimed at the onlookers. The clear sky over Turonia darkened in an instant.

"Now." Shalmar hollered.

Summoning everything inside them, Shalmar and Fernella released a flash of light from their palms. It crashed into Greenflack's magic midway. It was a standstill, one power trying to overcome the other.

Greenflack channelled more energy and began to push the energy back towards the sisters. It was getting dangerously closer.

"Fire." Harmish Greywater's voice erupted as he directed his forces to fire iced darts.

Greenflack was so blinded in his resolve to conjure up a spell to destroy the Amazon's and Turonia he didn't invoke one to protect himself again. The darts hit him squarely in his chest, he staggered backwards. Noieh began to fire her arrows in quick succession, adding to the attack. Greenflack used his residual energy to create a dome-like protection, but it was too late, he was too weak to stay focused. The arrows penetrated through the force field and punctured his arms and midsection.

Jacqueline and Redfear exchanged knowing looks and grabbed a couple of spears. They expertly took aim and hurled them towards Greenflack.

Shalmar saw Greenflack becoming more disoriented. The connection between the sisters was beginning to weaken, but she held on to hers and reeled more energy towards him. The darkness began to retreat.

"No" Greenflack screamed in agony.

Shalmar knew the connection of magic with her sister would soon fade, she breathed deeply and pulled the strength of the wind up through her in such a force that it lifted her off the ground. The air blew wild, lightening crashed igniting the sky above them, and it channelled its way down into Shalmar. Fernella felt the extra jolt of energy flow through Shalmar and into her. As it exploded from their hands, the sisters compelled the dark magic back causing it to implode in the centre of Greenflack's forehead.

Standing frozen, Jacqueline and her colleagues stood witness to this incredible act of power.

As the energy became far too hot for him to control, Greenflack felt his insides burn like molten lava. He screamed in pain as parts of his body began to skew off in distorted angles. As his body began to vibrate violently, what was left of him exploded and a flicker of light shot out towards Fernella. Jacqueline moved swiftly. She ran and leaped just in time to push Fernella out of the way. The light grazed Jacqueline's abdomen. The force strong enough to send her falling backwards. Greenflack had already turned to dust before hitting the ground and the gale had carried him away.

"No"

As Shalmar planted her feet back on the ground, she raced to Jacqueline's side. She took the young warrior in her arms and stroked the strands of hair away from her forehead. Every trace of her life force was drained from her, yet her body was glowing red with an unknown energy. Shalmar knew it had something to do with Declavius' magic.

"Jacqueline," Shalmar whispered, holding the slender frame of her partner. Shalmar herself was drained of her energy after such a fight. She had no power left to help her.

Everyone watched in silence as Shalmar studied Jacqueline's face. It became evident to the Elementals, especially Redfear, that this was Shalmar's primary mate. He had watched the white glow of energy that surrounded them when they were together. It was like a wave that encompassed them both. It was obvious to those who understood this type of union amongst the element people. It was not something that could be explained, it had to be experienced. Redfear wasn't even sure if Shalmar knew the importance of it, or if she understood that it was sanctioned between them. It was a conversation he promised himself he would have with her in the next days.

As they watched this red energy fluctuating and moving around Jacqueline, Shalmar gave space to it, unsure of what to expect. She looked at the chief hoping for answers. He only shook his head and looked confused.

"What of this?" Shalmar looked at Greywater. "Will she live?"

"I have not seen this before," his voice low. "It's as though his magic has put her in a trancelike state. I do not know what will become of it. We must wait and see."

Shalmar felt helpless. She was becoming angry at herself for bringing Jacqueline on this quest. She brought her back from the Chibanka and now this. She risked her life to save Fernella. Shalmar did not want to lose one to gain the other; in her heart, she knew it was Jacqueline's choice to stay or go onward. The silence seemed like an eternity as they watched the red-light dance around the body of the Amazon. After a few moments, they finally watched it fade. As she reached out to touch her, Shalmar began to feel a small sensation flowing from her partner to her and back. And slowly, heat began to return to Jacqueline's body.

"All be praised," Shalmar fumbled her words.

"Did we win?" Jacqueline struggled to open her eyes, giving Shalmar a weak smile.

Noieh grabbed a couple of herbs from her pouch and started tending to the flesh wound.

The air was suddenly pierced with shouts of celebration from every corner of Turonia. The few men of the Royal Elite Forces escorted the chief as he walked towards the warriors. A couple of them had begun to assist the injured men and carry the dead away from battleground.

"Turonia is saved," he bellowed. "We lost our children who fought gallantly to ensure that our city remains safe. While we rejoice in our victory, we must not forget the sacrifice that our people have made to secure it."

As he turned around, he saw his commander leading his wife and children to him.

Fernella had mixed emotions. For one, she was happy that she was saved with the help of her sister and her friends. She wondered how the families of the dead were going to cope with living a normal life now. It was not going to be the same. Also, there was Shalmar, the powers, the Amazons. How would the people of the Water element now feel towards those of Air? She was already lost in thought when Redfear snapped her out of her reverie, by touching her arm.

"You said you would come back," she said, smiling.

"I made a promise. I kept it," Redfear smiled. "Greenflack's tyranny has ended in Jadehollow. Your people are once again safe, your stepmother is seated back on the throne. She'll be delighted to know you're safe and coming home."

"Thank you for everything, Lambord," she threw her arms around him. As she pressed against the bruises on his chest, Redfear winced but he didn't let go. His hands wrapped her small waist as they held each other.

Their lips met in a brief dance. She disengaged from his grip. "I will be seeing you around then."

His sheepish smile was the only answer she needed. Redfear reflected on Shalmar's comment about his love for her sister. It still amazed him that Shalmar knew, and she knew that quick. Redfear also knew this strong woman before him, the princess ready to lay down her life to protect the people from Greenflack, was his primary mate. He nodded respectfully to Fernella and stepped away to help with the injured.

Jacqueline was back up on her feet, her wound covered by a mixture of herbs. Fernella trod towards them, her eyes taking in the three confident women before her—the realization that this was her family hit her. Noieh offered her a hand, and she stepped into the hug they shared.

After assisting with the wounded of Turonia, the sisters of the Air element started walking towards the shoreline.

"We have much to speak of," Shalmar broke the silence

With the help of the sun and water, the air smelled fresh again. The relief that Greenflack was no more was satisfying as the two examined the terrain before them. They took in the happenings of the day. Fernella heard the deep sigh from Shalmar and touched her sister's arm.

"She is okay, Shalmar,"

Shalmar looked at Fernella thoughtfully.

"You are Amazons. Some of the strongest warriors to set foot in these lands. If not by your side, Jacqueline would still be doing this. So, let it be as it is—by your side. You believe in her and who better to ride with you."

Shalmar smiled, understanding her sister to be right. Jacqueline was a fierce warrior, and at least together, they could watch out for each other. Shalmar sensed something was off but brushed it from her mind as she took in her sisters words.

"You must be exhausted."

Fernella could see how much effort her sister had put out and experiencing first-hand, even momentarily, the power she could invoke, she could feel exhaustion set in this powerful warrior. She looked at Shalmar, still amazed that this Amazon, the one whose name she had heard in stories from a far, was her sister.

Shalmar studied Fernella for a moment. She could see the wisdom in her eyes and feel the calmness she could gift to people. The bravery she showed in giving herself up to save the people of Turonia was truly impressive.

"Pray, tell, what was our father like?" Shalmar looked to her younger sister.

"Not until you tell me what our mother was like," Fernella jeered smiling.

# CHAPTER TWENTY-TWO

Sym sat behind the large table and reviewed the reports that Shalmar had presented to her.

Shalmar and Jacqueline stood still and watched Sym's expression go from mildly impressed, to bewilderment, even to sadness. Shalmar had specifically left out details about her powers in the description. It was not that she could not trust Sym. She just wasn't ready for anyone else to find out her true potential.

It had been six days since the battle of Turonia, and while Fernella convinced Shalmar to stay a while in Jadehollow, it was only for a short time. Blyst, and even the troublesome town of Rheyn, had always been home to her. It seemed fitting to accept the title of The Warrior of Rheyn in good stride. However, after helping Fernella and the queen restore Jadehollow to its former glory, they promised to cross paths more often.

"Well, this is impressive," Sym was drifting through the report. Attached to it was an updated map of the seas, which particularly pleased her.

"Well, you have fulfilled one part of the deal," the commander fixing Shalmar a knowing look.

Shalmar looked away. She remembered the deal she brokered with Sym before she ventured off into the vaults.

"I'm guessing your recruit doesn't know about the deal we made?" a sly smile on her lips.

"What deal?" Jacqueline's concerned look causing Shalmar apprehension.

"Well, she promised to accept my offer to become a member of the Supreme Council." Sym beamed.

"She did not," Jacqueline said, then realized that raising her voice may be a direct insult. She went silent.

"Actually, I did," Shalmar turning to face her. "The situation was dire, and I had to do what was needed."

"Shalmar, I have told you before that I admire your strong zeal and resilience. Taking up a higher responsibility in your service to the queen and Amazons would be quite delightful for me," Sym was rising from her chair. "But in hindsight, we need an experienced warrior leading the Amazons in the field. For now, no one can handle that better than you." She walked to the window. "I hereby place the agreement on hold. No one knew about it apart from us here, and everything will go back to normal. You have my permission to leave my office."

"Thank you, Commander," Shalmar stood, nodding her head.

"Leave now," she said, smiling. "Don't make me change my mind. It is only temporary, Shalmar."

Sym watched the two warriors through her window. She knew Jacqueline was more than a recruit. She had seen the loving way the two had exchanged looks on many occasions. The respect between them was evident. She remembered that feeling. Sym smiled fondly as her mind went back to the day, she and her lover, Miriam, had found each other. Miriam was from a place near Jadehollow, an area ruled by the element of Fire. She and Sym had met unexpectedly while Sym was on a quest. As she watched Shalmar and Jacqueline disappear into the Amazon quarters, she returned to her chair and allowed herself, for a moment, to linger fondly in the memory of the one who had captured her heart.

****

Back in Shalmar's room, the warriors lay tangled on the fur rug in a deliberate, easy release of desire. The moonlight seeped through the curtain casting a glow over the dim lit space. Their shadows danced on the wall in images of ecstasy, as they surrendered to the depth of emotions that had surfaced so powerfully with the experiences of these days past. The realization of being primary mate to Shalmar was deeply intensified in their release.

After they had satisfied their longing, Shalmar took a furtive look at the dark bruise—the result of Declavius' dark magic, on Jacqueline's smooth abdomen and closed her eyes briefly.

"You bear the mark of a warrior now," Shalmar teased, kissing the bruise affectionately.

"What was I before? A blacksmith?" Jacqueline smirked with an eyebrow raised. The room was filled with their laughter and it travelled with the breeze, blending in the night air.

# CHAPTER TWENTY-THREE

Inside the great hall, the mages gathered once again, encircling the fire, their head bowed. They had remained like that for several hours, none willing to speak the about the recent developments.

They had been quite hopeful after Declavius linked his essence to a lowlife who wanted to be ruler of Jadehollow. They were not impressed that the young mage had receded and granted control to the host. He was a brute who had a little idea of how magic could be manipulated to administer the worst damage possible.

"Declavius has left this realm, never to come back again," the chairman spoke again. "I, as well as you all, felt his essence dissipated. Our great return to civilization is no longer in the prospects for us."

He paused to gather his thoughts. "We must not fail to acknowledge that he exhibited great qualities and possessed powers very few of us here possess. It is a pity that the youngest of us all was the first person to venture into the afterlife.

"Declavius, before he died, left us a great ally. He transferred part of his magic."

Murmurs and unintelligible mutters filled the great hall, until the Chairman called for total silence.

"Here, look."

He clapped his hands, and circle they had formed turned into smoky mirror. They could see the small room and the fur rug where the two amazons were sleeping peacefully.

"We have control. I must figure out to what extent, but it can be used to our advantage," the chairman said.

Then, he faced the mirror. "Wake, Jacqueline."

They watched as the small bruise on Jacqueline's abdomen glowed red hot. Jacqueline's eyes opened, she seemed to be in a trance.

The devilish amusement of the mages reverberated through the walls.

They noticed her companion was on the verge of stumbling awake.

"Sleep now," the chairman commanded.

The slender frame of Jacqueline, eyes closed, turned into Shalmar, who pulled her close.

The great hall erupted in derisive laughter.

Thanks for investing in my book. It is much
appreciated. Feel free to leave a review as it does
help. I will do my best to continue to represent the
LGBTQ community in a healthy, positive light.
Be Well.
Serena

www.ingramcontent.com/pod-product-compliance
Lightning Source LLC
Chambersburg PA
CBHW030921060726
47591CB00005B/1624